"I hate this. Being scared all the time. Looking over my shoulder."

"I know. I'm sorry you're going through this, but I promise you, we will find this guy."

His words hadn't cleaned any of the concern from her eyes.

"You can't be sure of that. Certainly not sure that you'll catch him before he does something else. Something worse."

His gut clenched because, even though he meant every word, she was right. He couldn't be sure they'd catch the stalker before he lashed out again.

He let out a deep, steadying breath, then sat beside her.

"You're right. I can't promise you this guy won't send another email or more flowers or attempt another hit-and-run. But I can promise you that I will not let anything happen to you. I will stand between you and any danger. I give you my word on that."

A STALKER'S PREY

K.D. RICHARDS

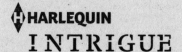

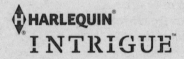

HARLEQUIN®
INTRIGUE™

ISBN-13: 978-1-335-59142-5

A Stalker's Prey

Copyright © 2024 by Kia Dennis

For questions and comments about the quality of this book, please contact us at CustomerService@Harlequin.com.

Harlequin Enterprises ULC
22 Adelaide St. West, 41st Floor
Toronto, Ontario M5H 4E3, Canada
www.Harlequin.com

Printed in U.S.A.

K.D. Richards is a native of the Washington, DC, area, who now lives outside Toronto with her husband and two sons. You can find her at kdrichardsbooks.com.

Books by K.D. Richards

Harlequin Intrigue

West Investigations

Pursuit of the Truth
Missing at Christmas
Christmas Data Breach
Shielding Her Son
Dark Water Disappearance
Catching the Carling Lake Killer
Under the Cover of Darkness
A Stalker's Prey

Visit the Author Profile page at Harlequin.com.

CAST OF CHARACTERS

Bria (Brianna) Baker—Actress, whose most famous role is Princess Kalvana.

Xavier Nichols—West operative.

Dane Malloy—Director of movie.

Mika Reynolds—Bria's agent.

Bennie (Bernard) Steele—Member of the paparazzi.

Rob (Robert) Gindry—Bria's old friend and costar.

Chapter One

Brianna Baker took a deep breath of crispy, New York morning air and picked up her pace along the Central Park path. There was probably another twenty-five to thirty minutes before dawn broke through the dark skies overhead and Bria wanted to be back at her Upper West Side townhouse before then. The morning air was invigorating and the forty-six-degree temperature was motivating, but the best thing about getting her morning jog in before the sun came up was that there was little chance that anyone would recognize her.

The brief snatches of time where she could be alone, unrecognized and just breathe and be herself, were what had kept her sane since her acting career had taken off and propelled her into celebrity status.

She wasn't complaining, at least not out loud. Acting had been her dream for as long as she could remember. And the fact that people, millions of people, thought she was good enough to spend their hard-earned dollars going to see her movies was thrilling and humbling in equal measure. But that fame had a price. The loss of her privacy for one. And lately, a nearly debilitating insecurity. The third movie in which she starred as Princess Kaleva, warrior princess, sent to Earth from an alien planet to retrieve the five elemental stones needed to save her people from certain death, had broken box office records in the US and overseas. She was officially an international superstar.

She was proud of the Princess Kaleva movies. They were showing little girls everywhere, especially little brown girls, that they were strong, powerful and smart and that they could be anything they wanted to be. But what she really wanted was to be taken seriously as an actress. But ever since she'd taken on the Princess Kaleva role, her agent had found it difficult to convince the Hollywood honchos that she could do the more serious roles.

Which was why she'd lobbied hard for the part of wife and mother, Elizabeth Stewart, in *Loss of Days*, a film about a family in crisis as a result of a child's drug addiction, when it had come up. It was a bonus that the majority of the filming, although on a tight six-week schedule, was going to be done in New York. In her heart, the city was still her hometown, even after fifteen years in California. It had taken some convincing and several auditions, but she'd won the part. And now she was weeks away from finishing the film she felt in her bones would prove to all of Hollywood that she could play serious, dramatic roles and not just be a busty superhero.

Princess Kaleva had pushed her into the ranks of celebrity, but *Loss of Days* was going to earn her the respect as an actress that she really coveted.

She picked up her pace. Although the sun had started to peek over the trees, the portion of the trail she was on remained deserted. She'd been jogging the same loop around the park since she'd come back to New York a little over a month ago to shoot the film. It totaled just over two miles and she wanted to make it the whole way before the park was packed with people.

She pushed through an uphill stretch of the path, her lungs burning. When she got to the top, she stopped, taking a moment to catch her breath.

Footsteps ricocheted off the trees behind her.

Bria glanced over her shoulder.

A figure jogged up the hill in her direction. From the size and gait, she pegged the person as male, but the shadows and a baseball cap pulled down low on the man's head obscured his face.

A bolt of unease shot through her. She began jogging again. She hadn't told anyone on her team about her morning jogs. Mika Reynolds, her agent, would have told her in no uncertain terms she was a fool for venturing out so early, and Eliot Sykes, her public relations manager, would have admonished her for jogging alone. But one thing she hadn't completely adapted to in terms of her recent celebrity was the complete and total lack of privacy that seemed to come along with it. And she wasn't sure she wanted to.

Bria shot another glance over her shoulder. The man was moving quickly, at more of a run than a jog, and with purpose.

She turned and began to sprint, less concerned with pacing herself than she was with getting to a more public space.

He's out for his morning run. He's not chasing you.

She tried convincing herself but survival instincts, honed over thirty-five years of being a woman in the world, pushed her forward.

She could hear the crunch of leaves indicating that the man was still behind her.

A level of fear she hadn't felt for a long time flooded her body, pushing her forward. She was still a bit of a distance from the entrance to the trail and she hadn't seen anyone other than the man behind her.

Without thinking, she plunged into the trees. Between the noise she was making crashing through the brush and the sound of her heart drumming in her chest, she couldn't tell if the man was still behind her.

She was probably overreacting. The man was most likely just another jogger out for a run, wondering why the weird lady had jumped into the woods.

But a voice inside her head screamed that that wasn't it at all.

She raced through the shadows, branches scraping against her arms and snagging her leggings. Darkness still clung to the dense woods, making her hasty decision seem ever more perilous.

She ran until her lungs threatened to burst, then crouched behind the thick trunk of a tree. She forced herself to listen past her own breathing for sounds that someone else was close.

She didn't hear anything she wouldn't have expected to hear in a thicket, but it was little comfort. If she stayed here and someone really was after her, had she just made it easier for them by darting into the trees? She had even less of a chance now of running into other people.

She couldn't stay cowering behind here forever. She pushed to her feet and plowed forward.

It seemed like it took forever, but finally, she saw the glow of streetlights.

Bria burst through trees, falling onto a walking path in front of a middle-aged man in a suit and carrying a briefcase. He started, freezing for a moment with wide eyes. She could only imagine what she looked like to him.

After a second, he rushed forward, concern plastered over his face for the wild woman who had literally just fallen at his feet. Thankfully, he didn't seem to recognize her. The last thing she needed was to have photos of herself online, leaves clinging to her leggings and twigs sticking out of her hair.

Bria assured the man that she was okay and didn't need an ambulance or the police.

He started away slowly, shooting a glance over his shoulder at her.

She attempted to smile, reassuringly only, but her eyes darted back into the darkness of the trees she'd just burst out of. She couldn't be sure, but it seemed as if the shadows shifted, taking the shape of a head and shoulders.

A car horn honked in the distance, tearing her gaze away from the trees for a moment. When she turned back, there was nothing to see but a solid wall of darkness.

Chapter Two

"I want to hire West Investigations, specifically Xavier Nichols, to provide for my personal protection while I'm here in New York." Brianna Baker sat on the other side of the conference room table at West Security and Investigations headquarters, the hem of her perfectly tailored skirt riding up high enough to reveal a silky smooth, caramel-colored thigh, sufficient to make a man's thoughts wander but not high enough to be tasteless.

Ryan West kept his gaze firmly fixed on her face. Not only was he a happily married husband and father, Ms. Baker was a potential high-profile client.

A potential high-profile client who was apparently familiar with Xavier Nichols, one of West Security and Investigations' best personal-protection operatives. A situation which was, in a word, interesting.

"May I ask who referred you to Xavier?" Ryan asked, not bothering to hide the note of curiosity in his voice.

Ms. Baker hesitated. "Let's just say his reputation precedes him."

It was all he could do to keep himself from laughing in her pretty face at that. If anything Xavier's reputation should have her running for the hills. He was good at what he did, protecting high-priority targets, but he had the people skills of a surly porcupine and communicated mostly in grunts and glances dark enough to turn lesser men to ash.

There was more to multi-award-winning actress Brianna Baker's story, a lot more if Ryan was reading her correctly. And his was a business that required him to be able to read people correctly. "Unfortunately, Xavier has just been placed on a new assignment. But, as I'm sure you are aware, West Investigations is the best in the business. I'm confident that another protection specialist can meet your needs."

"I'm sorry, but that won't work for me." She uncrossed her legs and reached for her handbag. "If Mr. Nichols isn't available, I'll have to find another way to solve my problem."

"One moment, please, Ms. Baker." Ryan held up a hand stopping her before she headed for the door.

She flashed a smile. "Please, call me Bria."

"Bria," he said with a nod. "Xavier happens to be in the office today. Why don't I call him in here and you can explain why you want to hire West Security and Investigations, and Xavier, specifically, to both of us."

She nodded, relief coursing across the delicate features of her face. "Yes, I think that would be a great place to start. Thank you, Mr. West."

"Ryan, please." He reached into his suit pocket for his phone, noticing as he did that some of the tension that she had been holding in her shoulders had faded away.

Brianna Baker was scared. And whatever it was she was afraid of, she believed Xavier was the man who could help her.

BRIA'S ALREADY RACING heart began to thunder once Ryan West declared that Xavier was on his way into the conference room. She was an actress, an award-winning actress no less, but right now, she couldn't find it in her to act as if seeing Xavier for the first time in fifteen years wasn't threatening to completely undo her.

She channeled her character from *Loss of Days*, Elizabeth Stewart, the matriarch of a rich, high-powered family. Elizabeth was always in control. She never let anyone close enough to read her thoughts or pick up on her emotions.

Be Elizabeth.

Bria took in a deep breath and let it out slowly as they waited for Xavier. She realized that Ryan West was studying her. She got the feeling he didn't miss much. That, she was sure, was what made him so good at his job.

She hadn't come to West Security and Investigations just because Xavier worked there, but if she was being honest, she would have at least checked out any private security firm he'd been employed by. Luckily, West was actually one of the best in the country. That was great because she needed the best.

Her stalker had gotten past every security measure she and her people had implemented to date, and if he really had been chasing her on her jog through Central Park earlier that morning that meant he'd followed her across the country as well. She was terrified of what he would do next.

So terrified that she was doing something she'd never thought she'd do. Turning to the man whose heart she'd broken and begging for his help.

Well, maybe not begging, but certainly asking for his help, which required her to swallow a heaping dose of humble pie. But it was worth it if West Investigations found her stalker and stopped the campaign of harassment he'd been on for the past six months.

And if she and Xavier rekindled something in the meantime…

No. Absolutely not. She wasn't there to rekindle anything. Despite the doubt that had crossed Ryan West's face, Xavier's reputation as a personal security specialist, a fancy name for bodyguard, was sterling. She wasn't embarrassed to admit she'd kept tabs on him over the years. He wasn't the kind of guy who had a social media presence, at least not one that she'd been able to find, and she'd deny it to anyone who asked, but she'd tried on more than one occasion.

But she knew he'd gone into the military after she'd broken up with him, become a decorated soldier in the army, then stepped into the private sector working as private security at West Investigations. He'd provided New York-area event security for several actors and actresses she knew. It had been easy to wheedle information about him from there. Actors were notorious for gossiping. And the actresses she knew that he'd worked for previously were more than happy to dish on the tall, dark and handsome bodyguard, even if he was more than a little surly. The surliness only made him sexier.

To that she could attest firsthand.

The conference room door opened behind her and she felt her entire body tense.

Ryan West stood, but Bria remained seated. She wasn't sure she could stand if she'd tried. Her back was to the door, but she could feel Xavier behind her. It had been like that since the first moment they met. Like they were on a special frequency, just the two of them. Whenever they were in proximity of each other, the air pulsated.

Xavier had yet to speak.

"Xavier Nichols, I'd like you to meet Brianna Baker."

Bria turned the chair and stood, facing her first

love, hell, the only man she'd ever been in love with, for the first time in fifteen years.

Fear, excitement and desire raced through her.

He'd changed over the years. He'd always been tall and lean, but now he filled out the dark jeans and long-sleeved gray T-shirt he wore. His shoulders were broad, his arms more muscled. His hair was still cut short, but the touch of gray just beginning to crop up around his temples gave him a slightly distinguished air. But the eyes, they were the same. Dark brown, just like his skin, that looked at her as if they could see straight into her soul. Eyes she used to love getting lost in.

Eyes that were gazing back at her now with open surprise and something else she couldn't put a name to.

"Bria." The sound of her name in his dark baritone swept over her like a warm ocean breeze at sunset.

She closed her eyes for a moment, remembering the last time he'd said her name like that. They'd been wrapped around each other in a dump of a rental house they'd gotten with a couple of friends in Atlantic City.

"Brianna." He said her full name this time and she opened her eyes, plunged back into reality. "What… what are you doing here?"

"Xavier, I need your help."

Chapter Three

Xavier stared at the vision in front of him. It took a lot to surprise him. He was a Bronx native, an '80s child who'd bounced from relative to relative and had seen his fair share of messed-up crap while doing it. And then he'd enlisted in the army, which had resulted in a whole new visage of nightmarish events.

But walking into West's conference room and seeing Brianna Baker, in the flesh, not just on a movie poster or in a commercial for whatever new film she was in, shocked him to his core.

He couldn't count the number of times he'd imagined, dreamed of what it would be like to see Bria in real life again. He'd played the meeting in his head thousands of times over the years, but none of those fantasies had prepared him for the moment he found himself looking into her beautiful brown eyes.

"What are you doing here?" He repeated the question. His brain was struggling to do anything other than drink in the woman standing in front of him.

She was gorgeous, even more so than she'd been

when they were twenty. The barest hint of makeup accentuated her warm golden-brown complexion and high cheekbones. Long, beachy waves cascaded over her shoulders. And her figure, a perfect hourglass. High, firm breasts and shapely hips that he longed to pull tightly against his body. Legs that went on for days, ending in the sexiest strappy black heels he'd ever seen. His mind instantly went to a vision of her wearing those heels and nothing else before he shook it loose.

"I need your help." Bria bit her lip, cutting into his fantasy. "West Security and Investigations' help."

He tensed and took a step forward, reaching out for her before letting his hand drop back down to his side. Damn. After all these years, he still wanted to wrap himself around her and protect her from every bad thing in this world. But he didn't have that right. Not anymore. So he went the more professional route. "What's wrong?"

"I have a stalker."

"Why don't we all have a seat and you can give us the details," Ryan said.

Xavier cut his gaze toward Ryan, only then remembering that his boss was in the room.

Bria had always had that effect on him. There was no one but her when she was near.

Bria sat back down, crossing her long legs.

His brain cycled to a memory that had him kissing up the length of those legs.

"Xavier." Ryan's voice pulled him back to the present. Ryan watched him through narrowed eyes.

It would have probably been more appropriate to move to the opposite side of the table and sit next to Ryan, but he slid into the chair next to Bria instead.

Ryan picked up his pen and held it at the ready. Every operative had their own style, but Xavier knew that Ryan felt taking notes by hand was less distracting for their clients during initial interviews. "So Bria, please, tell us how West Security and Investigations can help you."

"As I said, I have a stalker, which given my profession, isn't surprising. However, the stalker's outreach has…intensified over the last week."

Xavier's chest tightened. "Intensified how?"

Fear flashed across Bria's face for a brief moment before it was gone, replaced by what looked to him like rehearsed calm. "He, I say *he* because most stalkers are male, but I don't actually know if it's a man or woman, sent me flowers at my house." She paused for a moment, almost as if she needed to fortify herself before speaking the next words. "I get flowers from fans sometimes, so that's not the issue. It's that the roses were black. And withered. Dead. And the card that was with it was not like the usual fan mail. It scared me." A tiny shudder moved through her body.

Again, he fought the urge to reach out and pull her against his body.

"We'll need to see the note."

She pulled the compact rectangle of a bag hanging from her shoulder onto her lap and extracted a small card.

YOU ARE MINE. AND I'LL BE COMING TO TAKE WHAT'S MINE VERY SOON.

He handed the card across the conference room table to Ryan, looking up at Bria as he did.

She was trying to look calm, unruffled, but she'd never been able to keep anything from him. He could see the fear in her eyes and it ignited fury inside of him.

And terror. Because, even after fifteen years, if anything was to happen to her, he didn't think he could go on. His heart thudded in his chest.

"Do you have any idea who could be behind this?" he asked.

Bria shook her head. "No. Like I said, I get lots of questionable fan mail. The flowers were delivered to the set and a PA, a production assistant, signed for them and brought them to me. The PA didn't pay attention to the delivery person, and there was nothing with the flowers that indicated what florist they'd come from."

Ryan scribbled something on the notepad in front of him. "We're going to keep this note if you don't mind. Run a few tests on it. They'll probably turn up nothing useful, but you never know."

Bria nodded her assent.

"You said the flowers and this most recent note were a ramping up on the part of the stalker." Xavier rolled his chair a fraction of an inch closer to Bria. He might not be able to touch her, but he was damn sure going to stick close. "When did the stalker first get in touch with you?"

"It started with weird emails about six months ago, as far as we can tell."

"Who is *we*?" Xavier asked.

"I don't actually read my own fan mail, and it became too much after the first Princess Kaleva movie for my assistant to handle along with her other duties. Now I use a public relations firm. They read any fan mail I get and respond appropriately. Most threats are logged and never make it to my attention, but if the threat is deemed credible, I'm notified, as are the police and anyone else who may need to know."

"We'll need the name of the PR firm and whoever handles your fan mail there, as well as your assistant's name and contact information."

"That's not a problem. The PR firm is Eliot Sykes Public Relations. My assistant's name is Karen Gibbs. She stayed in Los Angeles because her mother is ill and she can't be away for six weeks, but I'll let her know she should cooperate and get you whatever you need."

"Thanks," Ryan said. "Now, can you tell us more about these emails?"

"They're anonymous, so it's hard to say for sure

that the emails and the flowers are from the same guy. The emails were weird at first but mostly harmless, so my PR team didn't even tell me about them initially."

"Weird how?" Xavier pressed.

A flash of something, hesitation maybe, went across Bria's face before disappearing just as fast. She pulled an envelope out of her purse and handed it to him.

He read each email before passing the printout across the conference table to Ryan. There were over a dozen of them. The first few were all some sort of variation on the same. "Your movies mean everything to me." "We belong together." "I'm your biggest fan." "No one loves you more than me." Pretty typical fan mail. But then the messages progressed to the more personal. Asking Bria out to dinner. To marry him. To have his child.

Hell no. The words screamed through his head. Even though he hadn't said them out loud he hadn't been able to beat back the growl that rumbled in his chest.

He focused on the emails again. Their tone grew even more possessive. "You are mine" and "We belong together" being the most popular themes, it seemed. Then the messages changed, but were somehow even creepier. "I'll keep your secret." "Don't worry. I'll never tell." "Your secret is safe with me, my love."

Not a threat, at least not implicitly, but they made his skin crawl just the same.

He looked up at Bria. "What secret?"

"I have no idea." Bria's gaze slipped away from him.

"This person clearly believes he knows something about you," Ryan said. "Can you think of anything he could be referring to?"

"You have to understand. This person might not even really be thinking about me as me. Lots of fans conflate the character an actor plays on screen with the actor themselves. This secret might be the secret of some character I played who knows how long ago."

Maybe, but Xavier didn't think that was it, and from the look on Ryan's face, he wasn't buying it either. There was something Bria wasn't telling them. But they could circle back to it later.

"The note with the flowers and the emails use slightly different language at times. The note doesn't mention your secret, whatever that may be, and it's an explicit expression of ownership and domination."

"I noticed that, but all the notes came from the same email address, so they must be from the same person. As for the flowers, it's too much for me to contemplate that there are two people out there stalking me at the same time."

It wasn't out of the realm of possibility, given the level of her fame, but there was no need to worry her with that thought at the moment.

"Have you spoken to the LAPD?" Ryan inquired.

Bria's face twisted into a frown. "Yes. They took a report but said there was nothing they could do. No laws have been broken and they didn't think the emails or notes were a direct threat. They suggested I hire private security if I was concerned."

Ryan's brows arched. "There are several excellent private security firms in Los Angeles. Why did you wait until you got to New York to seek private protection?"

A good question and one that Xavier should have thought of the moment she'd started explaining her problem. Bria should have had personal security the minute the tone of the emails had shifted.

He caught her glance in his direction before she focused all her attention back on Ryan.

"I was hesitant to take that step. I didn't want some creep forcing me to change how I live. Until this morning."

Xavier's heart rate ticked up as her voice trailed off. "What happened this morning?"

"I think someone chased me while I was on my morning run in Central Park."

"Why the hell were you running through Central Park when you have a stalker?" Xavier exploded.

Ryan cut him a hard look, but Bria spoke before Ryan could admonish him.

"Because it's how I clear my head," she shot at him angrily. "I won't be held a prisoner. You should know that up front. If West Investigations can't provide protection while letting me maintain my shooting schedule and some semblance of a normal life, I'll find a security firm that can."

Before he had a chance to tell her just that, Ryan held up both hands. "Hang on, both of you. Why don't you tell us about what happened in the park and we can go from there."

Bria explained that she liked to jog in the early morning to clear her head and because there were fewer people out to recognize her. She was out running on one of the paths in Central Park that morning when she'd felt a man coming up quickly behind her. She'd gotten scared enough of the man to cut through trees. She was pretty sure he'd followed her into the woods, but it had been too dark to see his face or any distinguishing features.

Xavier bit his tongue against the urge to admonish her for dodging through the trees. She'd increased her risk, darting into a secluded area. It was one thing to care more about her career than she did about him, but he couldn't believe she'd been so cavalier about her safety. Traipsing around New York alone and unprotected in the wee hours of the morning was just reckless.

"So you aren't absolutely sure you were being chased?" Ryan pressed.

Bria bit her bottom lip. "I'm not 100 percent positive but—"

Ryan held up a hand again. "I'm not doubting you. You did the right thing getting away from someone you thought could be a threat."

Bria's shoulders relaxed.

Unfortunately, every muscle in Xavier's body remained tense. "What about your agent and the producers of your movie? What's their take?"

Bria turned her gaze to him. "Be diligent. Watchful, but they aren't worried."

"But you are worried." Xavier stated the obvious.

"Look, I've been in this industry for over a decade. I've had my fair share of racist fan letters, creepy fan letters and even outright threatening fan letters. This feels different. And frankly, I'm more exposed here in New York, working on location instead of on a studio lot with tons of studio-provided security."

"So you would be paying out of pocket for your security?" Ryan asked.

Xavier shot a glare across the table at his boss. Money? That's what Ryan was thinking about? Who would foot the bill? Well, maybe that was his responsibility as the president of West Security and Investigations, but Xavier didn't care what it cost. Bria was going to have the full weight and protection of West Investigations protecting her 24/7 until they'd caught this sicko stalker, even if he had to pay for it himself. Something he wouldn't have had a hope in Hades of doing when he'd walked away from her fifteen years ago, but now it wouldn't be a problem.

He'd done well for himself working in private overseas security after getting out of the army and currently with West Security and Investigations. Not
only could he protect Bria now, he could provide for
her in the way that he'd only dreamed of when they'd
been a couple. The way she deserved.

Bria's back straightened. "Money isn't an issue.
A simple Google search will return estimates of my
net worth and I assure you even the highest number
is an underestimate."

Ryan held up his hands. "I didn't mean to imply
you couldn't pay our fee. I only wanted to get a sense
of whether we'd be working within the parameters
set by a studio or the producers of your movie."

Bria let out a long slow breath. "I'm sorry for
jumping to conclusions. No. No, if West Investigations decides it can take me on as a client, you will
be working directly for me." Bria cut a glance in
Xavier's direction.

"Consider us hired. As of right now," Xavier
growled.

Ryan frowned. "Ms. Baker has requested that you
be in charge of her protective detail and I explained
that you'd recently been assigned to another protective detail, so that might not be possible, but—"

"It's not only possible, it's done. I'll get Jack to
take over my current assignments."

"Xavier." Ryan's voice came low and authoritative.
Xavier met his boss's gaze straight on. He re-

spected Ryan West, and considered him and Ryan's brother Shawn among the few people he'd categorize as friends. But this was Bria. There was nothing he wouldn't do when it came to her safety. If he had to, he'd go it alone, quit his job, take on Bria's protection on his own. He still had a few contacts in the world of foreign private security and mercenaries. He'd pay them whatever it took to establish his own team, but frankly, he knew it wouldn't be the same as having West Investigations on Bria's side.

After what seemed like hours, Ryan gave a faint nod and Xavier started breathing again.

Good. West was the best chance they had of finding Bria's stalker and stopping him before Bria got hurt.

The mere thought of her being hurt had his gut twisting into little knots.

"Well, Ms. Baker, it looks like Xavier is available to head up your protection detail," Ryan said.

Bria exhaled audibly. "There is one other thing. The press hasn't picked up the fact that I've got a stalker. So far. I'd like to keep it that way for as long as possible."

"West Security and Investigations always protects its clients' confidentiality," Xavier responded.

A small smile of relief turned up the corners of her mouth.

An instant yearning to send that smile blooming wider speared him. He shoved it away. She'd made it more than clear fifteen years ago that nothing was more important to her than her career, including him, and he doubted that had changed. She'd come to him for his professional services and that was all.

He'd find the sicko stalking her and neutralize him and then they'd both go back to living their separate lives.

Just like she wanted.

Chapter Four

Ryan had his assistant go over the contract with Bria while he settled Xavier into his office.

"Okay, we don't have a lot of time, so give me the CliffsNotes version."

"We used to date when we were kids. She ended it. The end."

"She ended it."

"I'm over it."

Ryan's brows arched. "I can see that," he said sarcastically.

Xavier frowned. "I'll be fine. Bria's in trouble and I can help her in a professional capacity, so I will."

"And if your prior personal relationship gets in the way, you'll let me know, right?"

Xavier glared. "It won't."

"If it does…" Ryan pushed back.

Xavier nodded, then turned on his heel and went to find Bria. She'd just finished signing the documents that officially made her a client of West Investigations.

"I need to get to the set," she said when Xavier reentered the conference room.

"Your protection detail starts now. I'll take you." He led her from the room to the secure garage where West parked its small fleet of cars.

If he'd had his way, Xavier would have taken Bria to a safe house and squirreled her away until he came up with a comprehensive plan for her safety. Actually, he wouldn't have minded keeping her hidden until they caught the creep stalking her. But Bria had put the kibosh on any thoughts of a private refuge, temporary or otherwise, while her movie was shooting. So instead of heading for a safe house, he was driving her to the building where the movie was filming most of its interior scenes.

"Princess Kaleva made me a celebrity but *Loss of Days* is going to put me on the map as a serious actress," she explained on the drive to the set.

He made a right onto 42nd Street and drove past Bryant Park.

He shot a glance across the car, but Bria was focused on her phone and didn't seem to have noticed where they were.

They'd been all of nineteen years old when they met in this very park. He'd been heading home from his job as a stock hand at a grocery store in Midtown that no longer existed. Back then, he lived in a tiny studio apartment with a roommate, supplementing his income and picking up whatever side hustles he could to make ends meet. It was a hard life but he had never known anything else.

Cutting through the park, he'd seen Bria sitting on a bench, reading.

She was luminous. He stared at her for far longer than he should have before sliding onto the bench next to her.

She didn't spare him so much as a glance. He finally gathered his courage and asked her how she liked the book.

"It's a play. And I'm in it," she answered, with a smile that made his knees go weak.

"You're an actress."

"Well, I want to be. Someday," she'd responded boldly. "Right now I'm a student at the New York Acting Conservatory downtown." She looked at him expectantly.

He didn't have a clue about the New York Conservatory or any type of school, to be honest. Higher education had been so far out of reach for him he'd never given it a thought. "Sounds fancy."

"Well, it's not Juilliard, but it's a great school and I was lucky to be accepted." There was that brilliant smile again. "My name is Brianna, but you can call me Bria."

He took the hand she extended, and from that moment on, he was a goner. They'd sat on that bench talking, well, she talked and he listened, for another hour. And then he spent the last forty dollars he had to his name, buying her an early dinner at a local café.

They were together for a year. The best year of his life. Bria was kind and outgoing and he was gruff and spoke only when it was necessary, but somehow, they fit. What he felt for her, what they had together was deep, passionate. He'd never known anyone like her before. Never loved anyone like her before.

He'd realized early on that being with her made him want to be a better man. Her ambition had stoked his own, although he hadn't been sure what to do with it. Bria had opened his eyes to the difference between a job and a career that he loved. She made him think about things he'd never contemplated before. About right and wrong. About how to be a good person, a better person. About his future. He hadn't been sure about what he wanted to do for the rest of his life, but he knew he wanted Bria at his side and she deserved more than he'd ever be able to give her on a stock hand's salary.

Then one day, without warning, she'd ended it.

They'd met for lunch at a dingy café not far from her campus, which sold lackluster sandwiches at student-friendly prices. Bria was unusually quiet while they ate and the anxiety encircling her had knotted his stomach until he couldn't take it anymore.

"What is it? I can see something is bothering you," he'd said.

She dragged her gaze from her half-eaten sandwich to his face. "I think we should break up."

The words felt like a sucker punch to his jaw. "Why?"

"I got a part in a pilot. It films in LA. I have to be there right after graduation."

"That's great. But that's no reason to break up."

She reached across the table and grasped his hand. "Xavier, I love you. I do, but this pilot could be my big shot. I need to focus on my career. And your life is here in New York."

He squeezed her hand and pulled her forward so their foreheads met across the table. "If you love me, let's try to make this work. We can do the long-distance thing, and maybe once I've saved a little bit of money, I can move to the West Coast."

Bria closed her eyes. He watched a single tear drop trail down her cheek.

For a moment, he thought she'd agree. That he'd convinced her that their love was strong enough to overcome whatever hurdles life and her career might throw at them.

She stuttered out a breath and pulled away from him. "I'm sorry. I think this is for the best."

Emotions roiled through him, but his pride wouldn't let him beg. He'd stood, taken one last, long look at the woman he loved more than life itself, and walked out of the café.

Three weeks later, he heard that she'd moved to Los Angeles.

FINDING STREET PARKING was out of the question in Midtown, which forced him to park in a garage a block from the film site. He was vigilant in looking for potential threats as he led Bria to the vacant building that the production crew had rented to film the movie. The guard at the door took one look at Bria and waved them both through, much to Xavier's dismay. Lax security. They got a couple of curious glances as they navigated the labyrinth of the people and equipment, but no one questioned his presence.

Finally, Bria stopped in front of a door. "This is my private dressing room."

She reached for the knob and he quickly stepped in front of her.

"Let me go first." He opened the door, noting that it had not been locked. Not that the lock would be much deterrent anyway. A credit card and a good shove would overcome its resistance. The room was small. He could see at a glance there was no one inside.

Bria swept past him into the room.

"The security in this place sucks," he said, turning the flimsy latch. "I want to get you a better lock for this door and I want you to keep it secured. When you're inside and when you're not here."

She gave a brisk nod. "Okay." She turned back to her phone.

He got it. This was awkward. Things between them had not ended on a good note. But as long as she was willing to abide by his rules, they'd get along just fine.

Her dressing room was on a corner on the ground floor, a perk he assumed for the star of the movie. It had windows set high and running along two of the four walls. He tested the latches on the windows and determined they too were a joke. One good yank would be all it took for someone to force one open from the outside.

"The locks on these windows are no good either."

"I know. That's why you're here," Bria said, scrolling through her phone.

"I only saw a couple of security cameras, which isn't nearly enough for a space this large. And flimsy locks on the doors and windows."

Bria shot him an incredulous look. "We have security guards. I don't think it's that bad."

One of Xavier's brows arched. "You don't. I just walked right in, and despite no one knowing the first thing about who I am or what I'm doing here, I wasn't stopped."

Bria shot him a withering look. "You were with me."

His other brow went up. "And? Every single person in here should be wearing a badge identifying them as a member of the cast or crew. If they're here on an authorized visit, they should have a badge that says so. Security cameras should be recording 24/7, at the very least in the public spaces and at the entry and exit doors. I should call Ryan. Have him get our expert out here to work up a full security system." He grabbed his phone from his back pocket.

A laugh burst from Bria. "You're kidding, right? I mean, this building is almost a hundred years old. There's no way the owners are going to let you drill holes in the walls and run the kind of wires you'd need for something like that."

A low rumble tripped from his lips.

Bria smiled wryly. "I see your communication skills haven't improved over the years. Look." She set her phone next to her purse on the vanity and crossed to him.

She stopped close enough that he could smell whatever exotic fragrance she was wearing. Her scent had every cell in his body standing on alert.

"I don't want to tell you how to do your job, but you're not going to be able to approach this the way you usually do," she said, looking up at him with her gorgeous brown eyes.

He frowned. "If we did this how I want to, you'd be safely ensconced in the safe house while I tracked down this scumbag."

"And I've explained why that won't work for me." She threw her arms out to the side. "Don't you get it? This is it. This is my shot. No more wearing a skintight superhero uniform in movies that are more about my physical assets than my acting chops. This movie is great, and I'm damn great in it. Once the acting world sees that, I'll finally be taken seriously as an actress."

He closed the space between them and curled his hands around her shoulders. "Bria, there is no doubt in my mind that you are brilliant every time you step in front of a camera. You always have been. You have a gift. But it can't come at the cost of your safety."

His gaze was locked on hers. Heat crackled in the space between them. He wanted to kiss her so badly that it was a physical hurt. But he couldn't. Shouldn't. Getting involved now would cloud his judgment. He needed to be clearheaded, focused and—

All remaining thought fled when Bria went up on her toes and pressed her lips to his in a hot, rough kiss. A kiss that sent him hurtling through the past, and returning for a future with the woman in his arms.

Instinctively, he pulled her closer, deepening the kiss.

She made a little mewling sound that sent his manhood straining against the front of his slacks.

A knock sounded at the dressing room door.

Bria jerked back, her hand coming up to cover her kiss-swollen lips. She stared at him for a moment, desire still swimming in her eyes.

The knock came again. "Ms. Baker? Mr. Malloy would like to see everyone on set in five minutes."

Bria licked her lips and looked away. "Yes…o-okay. I'll be there in a moment." Footsteps faded away on the other side of the door. She turned back to him. "That can't happen again."

He was still breathing heavily and, he noted, she was as well. "Why not?" The question came out gruffer than he'd intended, but dammit, there was something still between them. He knew she felt it too. Why not explore it? See where it could lead.

"Because," she straightened to her full five-foot-eight height which was still a good six inches shorter than his six-two, "I'm here to work. I can't be sleeping with my bodyguard if I want people to take me seriously."

Her answer was frustrating in more ways than one, mostly because she was right. After all, he'd been thinking the same thing just moments earlier. But those moments in-between, when his lips were on hers and her body was pressed against his, had sent all rational thoughts fleeing. All rational thoughts but one.

"Why did you come to me?" He asked the question he'd wanted to ask from the moment he'd seen her sitting in the conference room. "Why did you come to West Investigations for your security?"

West was one of the best, sure, but there were other outfits that could have handled her stalker. Firms where he wasn't employed. But she'd sought him out specifically. If not because she still had feelings for him, then why?

"Because I trust you. Despite everything, you may

be the one person I trust most in this world. And I'm scared. You once told me you would never let anything happen to me. I'm hoping you really meant that."

He remembered that. They'd taken a day trip to Coney Island. He'd coaxed her onto the roller coaster, not realizing how afraid she'd be. She was shaking as the roller coaster car made its way up the inclined tracks.

"Don't worry," he'd said, wrapping his arms around her. "I'd never let anything happen to you. I promise."

Another, more insistent rap sounded on the door. "Ms. Baker? Please, to the set now!"

"Coming." She started past him.

He caught her arm. "I meant it then. I can back it up now. I won't let this stalker or anyone else hurt you."

Chapter Five

"Cut! That was great, Bria. Just great. I do want to try it one more time," Dane Malloy, the director of the film said.

Dane was a perfectionist. Usually that didn't bother Bria at all since she had more than a little perfectionist in her as well. But she was exhausted, physically and emotionally. Between her stalker, seeing Xavier again for the first time in years and doing the same scene now for nearly an hour, she just wanted to go home, slip into a warm bath and relax. But that was not to be.

They did the scene two more times before Dane was satisfied and let her go for the night. She walked back to her dressing room with Xavier so close on her heels that she could smell his spicy cologne. It sent a zip through her blood, cut through her exhaustion and almost, almost, had her catching a second wind.

She kicked off the four-inch heels she'd been wearing for the scene the moment she entered the trailer and reached around the back of her dress for the zipper.

After a minute of flailing, she finally gave up and turned to Xavier. "Could you help me, please?"

The smirk on his face was equal parts infuriating and sexy. "I was enjoying watching you, but yes, I will help you. Turn around."

She did as he said. There was nothing intrinsically sexual about what he was doing, but the moment his hands touched her body, she trembled with want. She recalled kissing him earlier and her heart raced.

His touch was featherlight and he lowered the zipper, slowly, much more slowly than was necessary.

She reveled in each simmering second.

After an electrifying, excruciating moment, Xavier's hands stopped moving. He stepped back.

Bria glanced over her shoulder. "Thank you."

Xavier's expression was unreadable. "You're welcome."

She headed for the small bathroom in the corner of the dressing room and quickly changed into her street clothes. After splashing water on her face, she looked at herself in the mirror. "Simmer down. He's here to protect you. Nothing more."

She looked at her reflection again. "Yeah, right."

There had definitely been something between them when they'd kissed. They'd never wanted for desire in their relationship. The overwhelming passion she felt for him was rivaled only by the passion she felt for acting. It's why she'd ultimately broken it off, because she couldn't see a way to sustain both, at least she hadn't thought she'd be able to do it when she was twenty years old.

The industry was hard and grueling. It took everything you had and then some to make it. And she'd wanted to make it. It wouldn't have been fair to Xavier to try to squeeze in a relationship with him between auditions and tapings. She'd done the right thing for both of them back then.

And now?

They were both successful adults. She could be choosy about her projects now. She could afford to take downtime between each film. Maybe they could make it work.

"Are you ready to go?" Xavier called through the bathroom door.

She shook the thought from her head and opened the door. "Ready to go." She slipped oversize sunglasses on even though it was far too dark for them already.

Xavier held her elbow gently and led her from her dressing room.

Between takes, she'd noticed him talking to Dane, several of the other actors, the set security, and one of the producers. She had no doubt they were discussing the lack of cameras and flimsy locks on the doors and windows.

She had no problem footing the bill for a few wireless cameras and latches but even celebrities had to budget. They'd have to discuss his plans later that evening.

The thought gave her pause. Her contract with West was for full-time security. But she wasn't comfortable with a stranger staying in her house. Xavier had been with her all day, but this was a job for him and he'd expect to have some time off. Another thing they needed to discuss.

It was late, but in New York, that just meant a change in uniform for the thousands of people still out and about. Instead of suits and conservative dresses with kitten heels, New Yorkers donned their going-out threads. Sparkly minidresses. Skinny jeans. Crop tops.

Bria kept her head down, hoping not to be recognized while Xavier deftly navigated them through the people.

They stopped at the corner of 42nd Street. It only took a moment for the walk light to begin flashing.

Bria stepped off the curb.

The roar of an engine cut through the normal roar of the city.

She froze. A dark sedan hurtled through the intersection, its grill pointed directly at her.

Almost as suddenly as the car appeared, her feet were off the ground and she was flying through the air. Because she still remembered every inch of his body, she instinctively knew that the brick wall that had slammed into her was Xavier.

He twisted himself so that when they landed he took most of the impact, hitting the pavement on his back and sliding for a fraction of an inch. Quickly, he locked his arms around her as he rolled them both to the far side of the street. Once again she found herself hurtling through the air, this time because Xavier had sprung to his feet, taking her with him and hauling her onto the sidewalk.

"Are you all right?" he asked, running his hands over her arms, his eyes roving over her body, looking for injuries.

Words escaped her and her mind struggled to catch up to everything that had happened.

Was she okay?

As if in answer, a sharp pain stabbed her in the side. Her knees buckled.

Xavier wrapped his arms around her waist, holding her up.

A young man darted up to them. "Oh, man, I saw the whole thing. That guy was crazy."

Xavier focused on the man. "Did you happen to get the license plate number?"

"No, man." The guy shook his head. "I'm sorry. It all happened so fast."

An older man hustled over. "Not so fast. That car was parked there for over an hour," he said with a smoker's rattle.

The younger man frowned at the older man, clearly

unhappy with being contradicted. "I don't know about that. I was just walking by."

Xavier's arm tightened around her. "Are you sure?" he asked the older man.

The man nodded. "I'm sure. I own this store." He jerked his head toward the bodega they were standing in front of. "I keep an eye on all the comings and goings around here."

"Did you get the license plate?" Xavier asked.

The man shrugged. "I don't keep that good an eye out. But I'll tell you one thing. That wasn't an accident."

Chapter Six

Xavier insisted on getting Bria off the public street, once he was sure she was unharmed.

"Maybe we should wait for the police," Bria said after they were back in his car and had pulled out of the garage.

"I'll take care of that when I know you're somewhere safe."

"You can take me to my house." Her hands still shook, but she was feeling somewhat steadier than she had in the moments immediately following the car's attempt to hit her and Xavier.

Xavier slanted her a look. "I need to take you somewhere safe."

"It is safe. No one knows I own a place in the city. I own it through a bunch of different LLCs. I even pay for a small suite at the Four Seasons when I'm in town to throw the tabloids off my scent. That's where the paparazzi think I'm staying while I do the movie."

Xavier still looked as if he was ready to argue.

"Please?"

He gave a grunt but said, "Where is this place?"

Bria gave him directions to her Upper West Side townhouse.

They drove in silence for several minutes before she could no longer hold back the questions. "The driver could have just been distracted, right? I mean, it might not have been intentional."

"That's possible," Xavier responded in a tone that made it clear he didn't believe the hit-and-run was an accident.

"But you don't think so."

He shot her a glance. "No, I don't. Even if the driver was distracted, there was time to swerve, but he didn't."

"But the stalker, he's been sending me notes, candies, flowers. Then chasing me this morning." Because she was sure now that she had been chased this morning. "And now to try to run me down. That's—" She paused, finding it difficult to get the next words out. "That's a serious escalation. Why would he want to do that now?"

Xavier shifted lanes, going around a slowing cab. "You've made several changes that could have induced the stalker to alter his methods. Leaving Los Angeles for New York, for instance. Hiring private security. The notes that you showed us from this guy are definitely creepy, but the most recent with the flowers was different. More aggressive than the others."

Bria shifted in the passenger seat so she was looking across the interior of the car at him. "More aggressive, how?"

"The 'you are mine' phrase was repeated, but the next line is even more aggressive. 'I'll be coming to take what's mine.' It sounds like there is some anger there. Anger, certainly possessiveness and a host of other things. The forensic psychologist that West Investigations uses may be able to help us there."

Her hands began to shake more violently.

Xavier must have noticed. He reached over and turned the heat on.

The blast of warm air was soothing and she was grateful for it.

Xavier eased the car to a stop at a red light.

"You know as well as anyone how much I've always wanted to be an actress. And yeah, I knew that there would be a downside to becoming a celebrity, but I'm honestly starting to wonder if it's worth it. I mean, how long am I going to have to look over my shoulder? Even if you find this guy, and there's no guarantee you will, there's always the potential that someone else will take his place."

A spark lit in his eyes. She'd always found his protectiveness sexy, and that hadn't changed. If anything she found it that much more seductive now. "And I'll always be there to protect you from whatever threat crops up. You have my word on that."

The light turned green and they began moving forward again.

Xavier navigated the busy evening traffic deftly, but it still took nearly a half hour to make it from the set to her townhouse on West 77th Street. She directed him to the garage at the end of the street. Like most New Yorkers, she didn't have her own car and therefore didn't need one.

He parked, then quickly led her to the townhouse.

Hers was the second unit from the corner, surrounded by a black ornate metal fence. Three stories with stairs that led to a large black door flanked by a series of narrow triple-paned windows on either side of the door. The front yard was small, but instead of paving over it as many of her neighbors had, she'd hired a gardener to maintain the small patch of grass and plant flowers in a miniscule flower bed. Although she owned a two-bedroom penthouse in Los Angeles, she considered the townhouse her true home.

"I'll want to take a look at your security system first thing," Xavier said while Bria worked the series of locks on the front door. She glanced at him, but his eyes were trained on the empty street, scanning it for the hint of a threat.

"Not a problem." Bria pushed the door open and led Xavier into the home's narrow foyer to a cacophony of beeps. She shut the front door behind them and engaged the locks before entering the six-digit code that neutralized the alarm and reengaged the security system. "It's a top-of-the-line system installed by Dustin Home Security Professionals. I spared no expense. I have a service that comes in to check on the house regularly. Since I'm away so much, it seemed prudent."

"Dustin systems are good. It's a brand that West Investigation recommends highly to our clients."

She kicked off her shoes and left her purse on the side table by the door. "Come on, let me show you around."

Xavier made a move to step in front of her. "Maybe I should clear the house first."

"Xavier," she said, unable to keep the exasperation out of her voice, "did you see what I had to go through to get in here? There's no one inside. Come on. You can clear the house as I show you around."

She'd purchased the house out of foreclosure six years ago with the check from the first Princess Kaleva movie. It had been a fixer-upper, but that was the only way she could afford a townhouse on the Upper West Side, even with a multimillion-dollar budget. She'd spent a year renovating, taking down walls wherever it was feasible and opening up the main floor as much as possible. Then she'd spent a small fortune on a designer who'd helped her give the space a clean, modern look while keeping a sense of hominess.

She led him into the living room, which flowed into the formal dining room before opening up to the eat-in kitchen and attached family room. Upstairs there were three bedrooms, one of which she used as a home office, and a bath in addition to the main bedroom and en suite bath. Back on the main floor she pointed to the door leading down to the basement.

"The basement is the only place I haven't gotten around to renovating yet. I want to put a full theater down there someday, but right now, it's unfinished. I keep the door locked."

Xavier tried the handle, but it didn't give.

"I told you. Locked." Bria headed toward the kitchen at the back of the house.

"It's a fairly open flow. You can almost see through the front windows from the kitchen here in the back," Xavier said. "The windows could be a problem. I want you to keep the curtains closed."

"They aren't typical windows. You can see out but you can't see in. I like my privacy."

"Still. Keep the curtains drawn at all times," Xavier said gruffly.

She blew out a sigh. "Sure. Want a glass of wine? I could use a glass of wine." She bent, reaching for the door to the wine cooler tucked under the island.

"I can't drink. I'm on the clock. Do you mind if I take a closer look upstairs and in the basement?"

"Sure, knock yourself out." She grabbed a bottle of white and straightened. "The key to the basement door is in the drawer in the side table in the foyer. I'm going to make mushroom risotto for dinner if that's okay with you."

Xavier's brow went up in surprise. "You cook?"

She laughed. "A lot has changed in the last fifteen years. I've learned. Eating out isn't as much fun with people asking for your autograph every few minutes."

"I can see how that would put a damper on dinner," he said, giving her a small smile of his own before heading upstairs.

Bria poured herself a large glass of wine, then got cooking. Risotto was fairly easy and quick to make, which was why she always kept the ingredients for it in both her homes. The food that was provided on movie sets could be hit or miss. They only had a few more weeks left of shooting and Dane seemed determined to make the most of them.

She could hear Xavier moving around, first in the basement, then on the second floor above her head while she prepared dinner.

It was surreal to have him in her house. Not that she'd never thought about it. A part of her had always hoped their paths might cross again one day. And that maybe their timing would be better. That some spark of what they'd felt for each other would still be there. At least she knew that part was true.

The spark was definitely still there, at least on her side, and she was pretty sure he felt it too. The circumstances were terrible, but she couldn't help hoping that maybe after they'd identified her stalker and neutralized him, they might find a way to start again.

Xavier came back downstairs just as she finished cooking the risotto.

"Perfect timing. I thought we could just eat at the island," Bria said, waving to the bar stools.

"That's fine, but before we do I want to give you this." He pulled a small device from his pocket. It looked like a key fob for a car but with a single button.

She frowned at the device. "What is that?"

"It's a panic button. I want you to keep it on you at all times. If for some reason we get separated, you can hit the button and it will send a signal to West's headquarters that can be followed."

She shot him a bemused look. "You're LoJacking me?"

"No." He tried to hide it, but she caught the slight upturn of his mouth. "It will only send a signal if you hit the button. If you push it by accident, you can hit it again twice, quickly, to turn off the signal. Totally in your control."

She took the device from him, her hand brushing along his. "I do like to be in control." The statement came out sultrier than she'd intended and she could see that Xavier had heard it that way as well.

His pupils were dilated and he looked at her with a fiery desire burning in his eyes.

She was on the verge of stepping forward and giving in to the kiss she wanted to press against his lips when he stepped back.

Disappointment flooded through her, but she pushed it away. "Let's eat."

She set the panic button on the counter and busied herself with piling risotto on two separate plates. She slid one in front of Xavier before placing the other in front of the empty stool and sitting down.

She hadn't realized how hungry she was until the earthy aroma of mushrooms and cheese hit her nostrils. She ate hungrily.

"This is good," Xavier said after a few bites.

"Don't sound so surprised," Bria teased back.

He smiled. "It's just that I don't remember you being that good of a cook."

She laughed. "Fair enough. Early on in my career, I did a straight-to-video movie where I played a chef. The movie was forgettable, as in so bad I hope anyone who saw it has already forgotten about it. But the production did hire a real chef to work with me so that I looked like I knew what I was doing. He taught me a few dishes and I found that I enjoyed cooking. It's relaxing."

"Seasoned with Love."

Bria felt her eyes widen with surprise. "You've seen it?"

"I've seen every movie you've been in," Xavier said quietly.

A surprising warmth flooded her at his words. "I doubt that. There were several early on that I wasn't even credited in."

"Every one," Xavier reiterated firmly, his eyes locked on her face.

She didn't know what to say to that. Did it mean something that he'd taken the time to watch all her work? Or was it just one old friend supporting another? And did it even matter?

Questions she wasn't sure she wanted to know the answers to. So instead of pursuing them, she changed the subject.

"Did you find everything you wanted? I mean, is my security up to your standards?"

"Your security system is pretty good. Better than pretty good actually, but there are a few upgrades I'd like to make."

"Whatever you think is best." Bria reached for her wineglass.

"I think it's best if you stay at one of West Investigations' safe houses."

She looked at him over the top of her glass. "Anything but that."

"Even if it compromises your safety?"

"I'm not just being obstinate," she said, setting her glass down on the countertop. "This is my home. It's one of the only places in the world right now

where I can just be me. Bria. Not Princess Kaleva.
Not Elizabeth Stewart or whatever other character
I might be playing at the moment. It might be hard
to understand—"

"I understand. I'm just…concerned."

He covered her hand with his.

A charge shot through her body. She wondered
if he felt it too.

"Thank you for being concerned." Her voice was
little more than a whisper.

Xavier pulled his hand back.

The loss of his touch felt as if she'd been thrown
into a cold bath. She grabbed her empty plate and
wineglass and carried them to the sink. "It's been a
long day," she said, her back to him. "I'm going to
head up to bed. Just leave the dishes. I'll take care of
them in the morning."

She hurried toward the stairs without looking at
him.

"Bria."

Xavier's voice stopped her before she got out of
the kitchen.

She stopped without turning around. "Yes."

"I'm… Good night."

His words seemed weighted and she wondered
if he was apologizing for more than just dodging a
kiss. But that was a conversation she was in no shape
for at the moment.

"Feel free to take whichever of the guest rooms suits you."

Bria hurried upstairs, shutting herself in her bedroom.

There was only one floor between them, but she wasn't sure the distance could ever be overcome.

Chapter Seven

Xavier was no cook, but he could do dishes with the best of them. He cleaned up the dishes from dinner and put away the leftover risotto. When he was done, he checked all the doors and windows in the house one more time. Bria's security was top-notch. He'd have expected nothing less from Dustin security systems, but he was taking no chances with her safety.

It was late, but he still put in a call to update Ryan on the situation with Bria. He'd spoken to one of the movie's producers and gotten the okay to have a security assessment done on the building as long as it didn't interfere with shooting. Ryan agreed to send someone to the set first thing the next morning to do the evaluation and change the locks on Bria's dressing room door and windows.

"How are the two of you getting along?" Ryan asked.

"We're fine. Just like I told you we would be."

Ryan's silence on the other end of the line spoke volumes.

"I need to get some shut-eye," Xavier finally said.

"Sure," Ryan responded. "Let me know when you need me to send relief. I know we argued for you to spend every moment with her."

"I'm not going to leave her until I know she's safe."

Ryan sighed. "I had a feeling you were going to say that."

They ended the call. He climbed the stairs to the second floor and paused outside Bria's bedroom. It was quiet and no light shone from under the door. She must have already gone to sleep.

He turned and crossed the hall, settling into the guest room directly across from Bria's room. He had an emergency go bag in the SUV, but he didn't want to leave Bria to get it. He slid the gun he'd had tucked into the waistband of his jeans under the pillow, shucked his boots and got into the bed, fully clothed.

An hour later he was still staring at the ceiling, wide-awake. The mattress was firmer than he liked, but that wasn't the reason he was finding it so hard to fall asleep. Every time he closed his eyes, he saw Bria step out into the street and the car bearing down on her. He could have lost her today. Lost her again, just hours after she'd walked back into his life.

He couldn't let that happen. He had to find the stalker and put him behind bars before he hurt Bria.

And then? Maybe he'd think about trying to convince Bria to give him a second chance. He'd been a fool at twenty, not to fight for her. Maybe they could have worked things out. But he'd let his pride get the best of him.

The irony of it was, some part of him had always believed they'd find their way back to each other. He'd tried telling himself that he was being a fool, pining for a movie star who had probably forgotten he existed, but the hope had never completely died out in his heart.

But now she'd come to him, needing his help.

A creak sounded in the hall.

His body went on high alert. He bolted upright on the bed and swung his feet to the floor. Grabbing his gun from under the pillow, he padded quickly to the door.

Pulling it open enough to peer through the crack, he found Bria standing in front of the door. He swung it open, taking in her purple-and-white-striped pajamas and the matching purple eye cover pushed to the top of her head.

"Bria? Are you all right?"

Lines burrowed into her forehead and worry shone in her eyes. "I just got a call from the night guard on the film set. Xavier, the stalker broke into my dressing room. He left another bouquet."

XAVIER PULLED THE SUV to a stop in the alleyway at the rear entrance to the building. Logan DeLong, the head of set security and a former New York City police officer, was waiting for them. Logan was a white man in his midfifties, with thinning red hair and a beer gut. Logan was one of the movie crew that Xavier had spoken to while he'd waited for Bria to finish rehearsals earlier in the day. Logan had given him a feel for the number of staff usually on hand, the security measures, and generally, how the production operated on a day-to-day basis.

"I'm sorry for calling you so late, Ms. Baker, but I thought you'd want to know about the intrusion right away."

Bria reached out and squeezed the man's hand. "You did the right thing."

Xavier scanned the alley. "Let's take this discussion inside." He hustled the guard and Bria into the building. They made their way through a maze of hallways that formed the behind-the-scenes area until finally stopping in front of Bria's dressing room.

The door was open and the lights on. A bouquet of black roses sat at the center of the dressing table, an envelope with Bria's name spelled out in block letters sticking out of its center.

Bria wobbled when she saw the bouquet.

Xavier reached out a hand to steady her. "You okay? You don't have to be here for this."

She shook her arm free and pressed her hand against her forehead. "I'm fine."

Keeping one eye on Bria, Xavier turned to Logan.

"Take me step-by-step through how you found the flowers."

"Well, the cast had left for the night by eight, but a few of the crew hung around to finish some things. Everyone had cleared out by nine. I completed some paperwork and was doing a walk through the premises, like I always do, to make sure everything was locked up tight before the night guard comes on shift."

Xavier nodded.

"That's when I saw the light was on in Ms. Baker's dressing room," DeLong continued. "She doesn't usually leave them on, so I went to check it out. Then I saw the flowers. Most of the deliveries go through my office, but I would have remembered black roses. The whole thing seemed...off. That's why I called you, Ms. Baker."

"Did you touch anything in the room?" Xavier asked.

DeLong shook his head. "No, I didn't even go in."

"Okay. You two stay here." Xavier stepped into the dressing room. Grabbing a scarf that was lying on top of Bria's vanity, he took the envelope from the flowers and opened it.

There was a photo inside but no note this time. The photo was dark and grainy. Obviously, several years old, but it still clearly showed Bria and another man at what looked like a campsite or somewhere in the woods.

He brought the picture to Bria. "Do you recognize this photo?"

Bria's face went sheet white.

"Bria? Do you recognize it?"

"It's from a movie shoot," she whispered. "A long time ago."

"Who's the guy beside you?" Xavier pressed.

"He was my costar. Derek Longwell." She looked at him with an unfocused gaze.

"Do you think he could be the one stalking you?"

Xavier had kept the explanation for his presence vague when he'd spoken to the head of security earlier, but now DeLong's eyes went wide at the mention of a stalker. Xavier ignored him.

Bria looked as if she was barely breathing and he worried that she might pass out.

She shook her head, her gaze finally focusing in on him. "No, it can't be. Derek is dead."

Chapter Eight

Bria woke up to the smell of coffee and bacon the next morning. It took some effort to drag herself out of bed and into the bathroom, and the image she saw in the mirror reflected that. Dark circles rimmed her bloodshot eyes. The makeup people would have their work cut out for them today. She let the water in the shower heat to just shy of scalding, then let it pummel her awake. She dressed and headed downstairs, feeling only slightly more human than she had when she'd awakened.

Pausing at the doorway to the kitchen, she watched Xavier at the stove, dressed in the same tight black T-shirt and blue jeans he'd worn the day before.

Her stomach did a flip-flop. Why was a man in the kitchen always such a turn-on?

Xavier shifted to look at her, his eyes skimming over her from head to toe. He hadn't changed so much that she couldn't read the concern in his eyes. So the shower hadn't helped as much as she'd hoped to make her look human.

"Good morning." Xavier's voice's husky timbre shot through her.

"Good morning."

"Coffee is ready."

"Thank you." She ripped her gaze away and headed for the coffee maker. "You didn't have to cook breakfast. We could have ordered something in."

Xavier spared her an elusive grin. "I may not be able to handle risotto, but I can manage bacon and eggs."

Bria carried her coffee mug to the island and sat.

Xavier slid a plate in front of her, then grabbed a cup of coffee for himself and sat down next to her.

He gave her a few minutes to eat before speaking. "You're going to have to tell me about it."

She swallowed the eggs in her mouth. "Tell you about what?"

After leaving the set last night, she'd shut down Xavier's questions. The shock of finding the photo had thrown her back to a time she'd worked to put out of her mind. She needed time to process, which she'd spent most of the night doing, hence the bags under her eyes. But she'd known Xavier wouldn't be put off forever.

"The photo. I saw how you looked at it in your dressing room last night. You looked afraid."

"How could I be afraid of a photo?"

He looked at her in silence.

"I told you. It's an old photo of me and a former costar."

"What movie?"

"*Murder in Cabin Nine*. It was a cheesy B movie that never got finished."

"Because Derek Longwell died while you were filming it?"

Surprise shot through her.

"I googled his name last night after we got back. Not much about him other than that he mysteriously died on the set of *Murder in Cabin Nine*."

"Yes, well." She swallowed again even though she hadn't taken a bite. "After Derek's death, the producers decided not to continue with the movie."

"How did he die?" Xavier pressed.

"I…I'm not sure. I think the official ruling was an accident. Derek drank a lot and I think they said he fell and hit his head." She couldn't bring herself to look him in the eye. After fifteen years apart would he still be able to tell when she was lying? But she didn't need to look at him to feel his eyes glued to hers.

"What aren't you telling me?"

The doorbell rang, forestalling her answer. Not that she knew how she was going to answer him. She couldn't tell him the truth. She hadn't spoken the truth to anyone ever and she certainly didn't want to tell Xavier. It would change the way he looked at her forever and she wasn't sure she could stand that.

"I'll get it." She rose.

He waved her back into her chair. "No. Let me.

We don't know who it is. You stay here." He stalked toward the front door of the house.

She bristled and followed him into the foyer.

He shot her a look that she ignored.

"It's my agent," she said, glancing out of the front window at the stoop.

Xavier opened the door.

Her agent, Mika Reynolds, jerked back looking stunned. "Who are you?"

Bria shouldered Xavier out of the way before he could answer. "Mika, come in." She turned to Xavier when he still didn't move. "Xavier."

It took another several seconds, but finally, he stepped aside.

Mika made no move to step into the house. "It's fine, Mika. This is Xavier. He's, well, he's my bodyguard."

"A bodyguard?" Mika frowned. "Doesn't look like he's doing that great of a job. You haven't answered any of my calls?"

"Your calls?" Bria grabbed her cell phone from the back pocket of her jeans where she'd slipped it after getting dressed. She had half a dozen missed calls and even more texts from Mika and several of the producers of the film. She'd never turned the phone's ringer back on after leaving the set. "I'm sorry there was an incident last night and I forgot to check my phone."

Mika didn't know the half of it. Bria hadn't even filled her in on the late-night flower delivery yet.

"Yes, I know. We need to form a plan about that actually…"

Movement behind Mika caught Bria's eye. A familiar form jogged up the walkway.

Bria felt Xavier tense beside her. "It's okay. I know him too," she said before turning back to the man making his way up the front steps. "Eliot! I thought you were in LA?"

Eliot Sykes swept her into his arms. "I grabbed a late flight out of LA to JFK."

"And I was already in town, taking meetings on behalf of another client," Mika said.

"You didn't have to come," Bria said, pulling free of Eliot's embrace. "Either of you. It was probably just a distracted driver."

"It wasn't a distracted driver," Xavier grumbled, "and can we take this discussion inside the house, please?"

Eliot kept one arm around Bria's shoulders as they stepped into the entry. "And you are?" Eliot asked after Xavier had secured the door.

"Her bodyguard," Mika answered from the love seat in the living room where she now sat.

"Bodyguard?" Eliot's arm tightened around her shoulder. "I thought you said you were okay."

"I am okay," Bria said, shrugging free of Eliot's grasp once again and putting some distance between them. "I told you both I was concerned about the notes I've been getting, and the flowers. There have been other incidents since I came to New York to start filming." She filled them in on the most recent notes, being chased on her jog in the park and the flower delivery last night, but left out the photo of her and Derek. As far as she was concerned, the fewer people who knew about that, the less explaining she'd have to do. Or avoid doing, as she currently was with Xavier. "I thought it was best to have personal security, so I went to West Security and Investigations. This is Xavier Nichols. Xavier, this is Mika Reynolds, my agent, and Eliot Sykes. He owns the firm that handles my media and public relations."

Bria walked to the love seat and sat down next to her agent. There wasn't enough space for Eliot to sit too, so he took a seat on the larger sofa in the room. Xavier placed himself at the far end of the living room, leaning against the wall.

Mika's face scrunched as if she'd smelled something foul. "The notes and flowers again. I told you it was nothing to worry about." Mika waved a hand in front of her face as if shooing away a gnat. "All the big stars have exuberant fans. It's almost a rite of passage."

Irritation bubbled in Bria's chest. Mika was one of the best agents in the business because she was laser focused on helping her clients build their careers, but sometimes her focus could be shortsighted. "It's a rite of passage that concerns me, then. We can't be sure whoever is sending them is harmless. My intuition is saying that whoever is doing this is serious, and even though the near hit-and-run could have just been a reckless driver…"

"I think hiring a bodyguard is the right way to go. Especially with this video making the rounds now," Eliot said.

"What video?" Xavier barked, pushing away from the wall and moving back to Bria's side.

Mika already had her phone in her hand. She tapped it twice, then turned the screen so that Bria and Xavier could see it. "Your bodyguard pushing you out of the way, rescuing you from the out-of-control vehicle. It's all over social media." She flicked a glance in Xavier's direction.

Bria watched herself freeze in the middle of the street, trapped in the glare of the white headlights bearing down on her. Her heart rate picked up, remembering the moment, even though there was no way she could be hurt by the vehicle while she was sitting on the sofa in her home. Then Xavier entered the frame, pushing her out of the way. The car roared past them and the recording froze on her and Xavier lying on the sidewalk, Xavier cradling her, staring down at her, his face a mask of concern.

"You can't buy this kind of exposure for the movie." Mika's excited voice cut through the memories.

Bria looked at the woman who'd been her agent for the last decade, who'd taken her on and helped make her into a star. It was as if she was looking at

Mika for the first time and she wasn't sure she liked what she was seeing. "We could have been killed."

Mika had the grace to look abashed. "Of course, I'm glad no one was hurt. That goes without saying."

Did it though? Bria couldn't help but feel like it was something that should be said.

"But it is undeniable that this will bring more attention to the film. And that's what we want."

Bria felt the frown she wore deepen.

"I think what Mika is trying to say in her characteristically tactless way is that we can use this incident to get some buzz for the movie." Eliot held his hands up as if to ward off an impending verbal attack. "I know how slimy it sounds, but this is the business. People are talking about your brush with death. We want them talking about *Loss of Days* and how brilliant you are in it and how it is going to make you an even bigger star."

"And maybe even garner some awards buzz." Mika did a little dance on the love seat next to Bria, her face glowing.

Bria glanced at Xavier, but his expression gave nothing away. She really wished she knew whether he was thinking that taking advantage of their near miss was an opportunity or opportunistic. "It sounds like a tasteless move to me."

Eliot slid to the end of the sofa closest to the love seat and reached across the sofa arm for Bria's hand. "It won't be. I promise. Don't I always take care of you? You're my best client and I'd never put you in an uncomfortable situation, but I do think a few strategically granted interviews right now, about the movie of course, wouldn't be a bad idea."

"About the movie? *Loss of Days* won't be out for another year at least. We haven't even finished filming."

"You should know better than that by now," Mika scolded. "It's never too early to start promoting a movie."

"How many interviews?" Bria asked.

"Three or four, tops," Eliot answered. "Just enough to make sure we're in control of the story. We want people to know you didn't suffer any injuries and that you were back at work the next day, ready to go on with this fantastic movie that everyone should see when it comes out."

"Okay," she said resignedly. "Two interviews. That's it, Eliot. I'm still filming, I don't have a lot of spare time."

Eliot beamed. "Great." He sprung from the sofa. "I'm going to get on that right now. It'll give you and Mika some time to discuss a few things."

Eliot strode from the room in the direction of the kitchen, already pulling his phone from his suit pocket.

The show must go on. Wasn't that what they said, she thought wearily. She only wished she wasn't a part of this madman's show.

Chapter Nine

Sykes was on the phone, his back turned when Xavier walked into Bria's kitchen. He studied the man for a moment. Sykes wore a fitted suit in a deep plum shade with a black silk shirt. A goatee dusted his chin and a Rolex watch encircled his wrist.

Finally sensing he wasn't alone, Sykes turned.

Xavier walked nonchalantly to the sink, took a glass from the shelf above it and filled it with water from the tap. He turned, sipping from the glass and watched Sykes.

Sykes's eyes narrowed when he realized that Xavier wasn't going to leave the room. "Excuse me, Ian. I'm going to need to phone you back." Sykes ended the call. "Can I help you with something?"

"You can. You can help by telling me about your relationship with Bria." Xavier leaned back against the counter, effecting a relaxed pose although his muscles were taut and he remained watchful.

"Bria is a client of my public relations firm. And a good friend. A very good friend." Sykes smirked.

Xavier knew Sykes was trying to get under his skin. Unfortunately, it was working. He itched to wipe the smirk off the man's face and tell him how his close friend Bria had pulled him into a smoldering kiss in her dressing room a day earlier or the ripples of desire that moved between them with every look. But letting Sykes get to him would give the man the upper hand.

"That so? Bria never mentioned you, but she always did tend to see the good in everyone. Even those who may not deserve it."

Sykes's eyes narrowed. "Always? So you aren't just some meatheaded bodyguard she hired yesterday?"

"Let's just say we go way back and are also very good friends."

He knew it was petty, but he couldn't help being pleased by Syke's scowl.

"I understand that your firm has taken over handling Bria's fan mail. I need to see everything you have."

"As long as Bria consents, you'll have it."

"How does it work? Does everything come to your firm directly?"

Sykes shrugged. "Most fan interactions occur online nowadays. Email and social media. The case manager assigned to Bria's account responds to the fans and flags the questionable stuff."

"What does the case manager do with the flagged communications?"

"Sometimes nothing. You'd be amazed how much negative stuff comes in. If it doesn't seem like a credible threat, well, we don't have the bandwidth to follow up on everything."

"And when you do get a credible threat?"

"We let the appropriate people know. Mika." Sykes's chin jutted toward the living room. "On-set security if she's working on a movie. And the police, if we deem that necessary."

"Not Bria?"

Sykes nodded. "We let her know too when there is a threatening message, although she has chosen to retain access to all her accounts and does still occasionally respond directly to fans." The expression on Sykes's face made it clear he didn't agree with that choice.

"And you notified the LA police department about the stalker's emails? The ones declaring that Bria was his?" Xavier continued his questioning.

Sykes shifted uncomfortably. "Not at first. I mean, there was no concrete threat. It wasn't the first time Bria got an email from a lovesick fan. No one thought the guy was a stalker. Not at first."

"When did you realize the notes were coming from more than just a lovesick fan?"

"When the black roses arrived at Bria's house. She freaked out and I can't say I blame her."

"And that's when the police were called?"

"Yes." Sykes flipped his phone front to back, back

to front nervously in his right hand. "Not that they did anything about it. In fairness, if they followed up on every threat to every Hollywood actor and actress, they wouldn't have time to do anything else."

Maybe. But he didn't care about every actor or actress. He only cared about one.

"Did anyone follow up on how the flowers got to Bria's house?"

Sykes's eyebrows squished together. "What do you mean?"

"Did anyone try tracking down the florist the flowers came from? Look into who delivered the roses?"

"I don't know." Sykes frowned. "I assumed the police would have done that."

"But no one followed up with the LAPD?"

Sykes shrugged again. "I guess not."

Xavier didn't try to hide his annoyance that there'd been so little follow-through initially, but it was something that he'd be sure to remedy, although the trail was probably stone-cold at this point.

"I really wish I could help you more," Sykes said.

"I bet you do," Xavier said without making an attempt to hide his derision.

Sykes frowned. "Look, I want to keep Bria safe as much as you do. Despite what you may think, I'm glad she hired you. Well, maybe not you but that she hired personal security. If there's anything I can do to catch the guy who is stalking her, I'll do it. But at the moment, I need to get back to work. So if you don't have any more questions…"

"I don't for now."

Sykes swept past him. Xavier followed Sykes back into the living room.

Bria looked from one man to the other. "Everything okay?"

"Fine," Sykes assured her.

"I set up the first interview with Ian Cole. I'll send you the details once I've worked them all out. Mika has your shooting schedule?"

"Yes." Bria nodded. "I have some time off coming up, so that would be the best time to do it."

"Great." Sykes smiled. "I'll let you know ASAP."

"Now, speaking of my schedule—" Bria rose from the love seat "—I need to get ready and head to the set. I'm lucky I don't have an early call time today, but I don't want to be late."

Mika and Eliot rose and headed for the door. Mika said a quick goodbye before pulling out her phone and heading for a black town car idling on the other side of the street.

Xavier bristled when Eliot stopped just outside the door and pulled Bria into another embrace. "I'm going to be in town for a few days staying at my place in Chelsea. Let's have dinner tonight." He shot a look over her shoulder at Xavier. "Alone."

"I don't know, Eliot. I'll have to see how filming goes."

Eliot's mouth turned up in a smile that didn't reach his eyes. "I'll call you later, then." He followed Mika to the town car.

Bria shut the door and turned back to Xavier.

"Nice friends you got there," he said before turning his back to her and heading for the kitchen.

"You don't even know them. They are an important part of my team. Mika is one of the best agents in the business and she's been a good friend to me. And Eliot has gone above and beyond, helping me handle everything with the stalker."

Xavier frowned. "You're right. I don't know them. But maybe you should consider this. Many stalkers know their victims personally. So maybe you should ask yourself how well you really know your team."

THE MOVIE DIRECTOR, Dane Malloy, called, "Action," and Xavier watched Bria become Elizabeth Stewart, matriarch of a not-so-upstanding political dynasty. She took control of the scene and demanded attention. Bria really was a damn good actress. Better than good. She'd been good fifteen years ago when she was a student, but now Xavier couldn't take his eyes off her. Admittedly, her acting chops weren't the sole reason for that. That kiss they'd shared had been brief but soul stirring. And he was determined to do it again. Soon.

"She's good." Ryan's familiar voice came from behind him.

Ryan held a tablet Xavier recognized as one they used when they were on-site conducting security reviews for clients.

"I didn't expect you to come out to do the assessment yourself."

Ryan shrugged. "I've never been on a movie set. Couldn't pass up the opportunity."

After Sykes and Mika Reynolds's unexpected visit this morning, he'd forgotten to let Logan DeLong know to expect someone from West Investigations would be coming by to do the security review. "How'd you get on set?" Xavier asked.

"Yeah, security around here is crap. I just told them I was with you and showed my West Investigations employee ID and they let me right through."

Xavier glared at the backs of the security guards, fifty yards or so away, who were supposed to be keeping the set secure. Frustration rumbled in his chest. He'd have to have another chat with Logan DeLong. And maybe get Bria to ask her bulldog of an agent to make a fuss to the producers of the film. After all, if anything was to happen on set, the lax security would be a huge potential liability for them.

He made a mental note, then turned back to Ryan. "Find any fingerprints on the vase of flowers?"

"Nothing," Ryan said. "Guy must have worn gloves. I did get the video from one of the few security cameras. Of course, I'd have twice as many around the set as they do, but at least they do have a couple of cameras. One caught our guy." Ryan pulled out his phone, and moments later, video began playing on screen.

A figure, clearly a man from the shape and size, walked into the frame carrying the vase of flowers he and Bria had found in her dressing room last night. The man kept his head down, and the baseball cap he wore obscured any hope of making out distinguishing features. But the vase of flowers in his hands was clear, as was the fact that he wore gloves. He was in and out of the frame in less than five seconds.

"None of the guards remember letting a delivery guy on set, but…" Ryan let the sentence trail off.

Xavier didn't need him to finish the thought. His tour of the movie set had revealed a number of weak points. Like the fact that there were multiple doors in and out of the building. The official entrance and exit that all cast, crew and visitors were supposed to use were manned. The other doors couldn't be opened from the outside but anyone inside could leave through them. Which meant they could accidentally or intentionally let a stranger on set without going through security, such that it was.

Ryan tapped the phone's screen, and less than a second later, Xavier's phone beeped with an incoming message. "I sent it to you. The techs at West are working on cleaning it up to see if we can get anything more from it, but they aren't hopeful. I've got someone following up with local flower shops here and in Los Angeles, where the first bouquet was delivered, but that's looking for a needle in a haystack."

Xavier wasn't surprised about that. He'd filled Ryan in on the lack of follow-up after the arrival of the first bouquet while Bria got ready to drive over to the set that morning. Neither of them held out much hope this would be a fruitful line of inquiry, but it was legwork that had to be done.

"We'll look anyway." Xavier turned his gaze back to Bria.

Bria chatted with her costar while the crew reset the scene.

"Anything on Derek Longwell?" Xavier asked without taking his eyes off Bria.

"Not a lot. I emailed you what we've got. He was a small-time actor living in LA. Only had a handful of credits when he died on the set of a movie filming in the San Bernardino National Forest a little over ten years ago."

"*Murder in Cabin Nine.* Bria was his costar," Xavier said. "What's the official word on how Longwell died?"

"Cracked skull. He had a blood alcohol level of .17."

"So, sloppy drunk."

"Exactly," Ryan confirmed. "We know he was out with some of the cast members at a local bar. No one remembers him leaving, but everyone agreed Derek was drinking heavily that night. The police theorize that Longwell fell along the path heading back to the hotel and hit his head. He wasn't found until the next morning when he didn't show up to the set."

Xavier turned the information over in his head. "So why would Bria's stalker leave a photo of Bria and Longwell with the flowers?"

Ryan jutted his chin in Bria's direction. "Have you asked Bria?"

"She said she didn't know."

"You don't believe her?"

"She's not telling me something, but if I push her too hard, she might dig in even more. She's got a stubborn streak," he said, thinking about Bria's refusal to go to a safe house.

One of Ryan's brows rose. "You may have to. The stalker left that photo for a reason, which means we need to know everything there is to know about Bria's relationship with Derek Longwell."

The idea that there was a relationship between Bria and Derek Longwell, or anyone else, made him want to punch someone. Maybe several someones. Of course, it was unrealistic to expect that Bria had remained celibate for the last fifteen years. He certainly hadn't. But that didn't mean he wanted to know the specifics of her relationships.

"So, you and Brianna Baker. I knew you were a man who kept his own council, but that's a pretty big secret to keep."

Xavier slid a side long look at his friend. "Wouldn't

you keep it to yourself if the best thing that ever happened to you dumped you like a hot potato?"

Ryan nodded sagely. "I probably wouldn't be screaming it from the rafters. I see your point." Ryan was quiet for a beat. "So, the best thing that ever happened to you?"

Xavier grumbled. He considered Ryan a friend, a good one, but that didn't mean he wanted to share his feelings with him. Especially when he wasn't sure about those feelings himself.

Ryan chuckled then sobered. "Look, man, I get it. The right woman can make us go a bit nuts, but Bria, she may be in some real trouble here. Her stalker is getting bolder. Sneaking onto the movie set, even after the shooting had wrapped for the day, was a big risk. Are you sure you can keep your head in the game?"

Xavier turned to look at Ryan head on. "Would you trust anyone other than yourself with Nadia's safety if the situation was reversed?" he asked, referring to Ryan's wife.

Ryan didn't hesitate this time. "No." He sighed. "Just let me know if you need anything. I'm headed back to the office to work on the cost estimate for the upgraded security suggestions." He dropped a set of keys in Xavier's hand. "I took care of the locks on Bria's dressing room door and windows and installed a wireless camera outside the door."

"Thanks, man."

Ryan patted him on the shoulder, then headed for the exit.

Another hour passed before the director finally called for a break for lunch.

A production assistant handed Bria her robe. She wrapped it around herself as she made her way to him.

"Was that Ryan I saw you talking to?"

Xavier fell into step beside her and they headed for her dressing room. "Yes. He did the security assessment, changed your locks and gawked at a real-life movie being filmed."

Bria smiled. "Tell him to let me know when he has some time and I'll give him a proper tour."

They arrived at her dressing room, but Bria hesitated. He read the anxiety in her eyes.

"Hey." He pointed to the camera Ryan had hooked up on the opposite wall from the dressing room door. "No one has been in or out since we left."

Bria took a deep breath and unlocked the door with the key he passed to her.

Inside, she fell onto the sofa. "I hate this. Being scared all the time. Looking over my shoulder."

"I know. I'm sorry you're going through this, but I promise you, we will find this guy."

His words hadn't cleaned any of the concern from her eyes.

"You can't be sure of that. Certainly not sure that you'll catch him before he does something else. Something worse."

His gut clenched because, even though he meant every word, she was right. He couldn't be sure they'd catch the stalker before he lashed out again.

He let out a deep, steadying breath, then sat beside her.

"You're right. I can't promise you this guy won't send another email or more flowers or attempt another hit-and-run. But I can promise you that I will not let anything happen to you. I will stand between you and any danger. I give you my word on that."

He wasn't sure who initiated it, maybe they both had. But in an instant, he was lowering his head to meet her raised lips. The moment their lips met, an electrical charge flowed through him.

Her lips parted beneath his and he took it as a sign and deepened the kiss. Her hands slid around his neck and he pulled her closer.

He'd known he'd wanted her the moment he'd seen her in Ryan's office, but the kiss just made it crystal clear how deeply he felt for her. He was throbbing with his need to be closer to her. And from the way she was kissing him back, she felt the same.

A ding sounded from the counter where Bria had left her phone while she was on set. She broke off the kiss, rising from the sofa and covering her swollen lips with a hand before turning her back on him.

"That was a mistake. Totally unprofessional of me."

"It might have been unprofessional of both of us, but I don't think for a second it was a mistake. Bria,

I think we should talk about what happened between us—" He broke off when her body tensed. "What? What is it?"

He stood and closed the short distance between them.

Bria turned to face him, her face full of fear. She held her phone out to him. "He…he sent me a text. It's you."

Xavier took the phone from Bria's hand. On the screen was a photo of Xavier with his arm around Bria, hustling her from the movie set into his SUV. A red circle with a slash through it had been superimposed over his face. The text underneath the photo read:

GET RID OF HIM. OR I WILL.

Xavier took a screenshot of the text, then sent it to his own phone. Then he pressed the call button on Bria's screen.

Alarm flashed over Bria's face. "You're calling him? You can't call him."

Xavier led her back to the sofa. "Don't worry. I've got this."

The phone rang, but no one picked up. It was a long shot. Just like tracing the number was a long shot. More than likely the stalker was using a burner phone. But that wouldn't stop him from trying.

He ended the call and started another. "We might be able to trace this."

Ryan wouldn't have made it back to West's headquarters yet, so Xavier tried Shawn, Ryan's younger brother and co-owner of West Security and Investigations.

Shawn picked up on the second ring, and after a brief explanation, set out to trace the number that had just sent the text to Bria's phone.

"Shawn is on it," he said, punching off the call, "but it could take a while. Are you finished with filming for the day?"

Bria shook her head. "No, I've got another scene to shoot."

Damn. He'd hoped to be able to take her home, but he knew she wouldn't leave the cast and crew in the lurch.

"Xavier, I'm scared." Fear pulsed off her.

He reached out and pulled her into his arms. He dropped a kiss on the top of her head. "I know, but we're going to find this guy and stop him. I promise you that."

Chapter Ten

For the next three hours, Xavier prowled the edges of the set, never taking his eyes off Bria and the people around her. He'd always known how talented she was, but now he was getting a glimpse at just how much of a dedicated professional she was as well. The text message had clearly upset her, but she pulled herself together and headed back to the movie set when the production assistant called for her. She acted the scene over and over, never missing a line.

Over the course of the next several hours, she filmed scene after scene without letting on how shaken she was. Of course, he could see it. In the nervous glances around the set between takes and in the way her eyes sought him out the moment the director called cut. He made sure to stick as close to her as he could, both so that he could keep an eye on her at all times and to give her the sense of security that she seemed to need at the moment.

The notes and flowers were terrorizing for Bria, but until now, the stalker hadn't exhibited a direct desire to physically harm her or anyone else. But the text message with his photo, along with the attempted hit-and-run, couldn't be taken as anything other than a direct threat against them. An escalation in the stalker's MO. He wasn't scared for himself, he was scared for Bria. Because there was no way he was leaving Bria's side, which meant the stalker might escalate even further. And there was no way to guess what he might do next.

While Bria worked, Shawn called to fill him in on the attempt to trace the text message. The techs at West had done their best to locate a name or location for the call, but not surprisingly, the message had come from a burner phone. The device was currently off or disabled, so unless the stalker used it again, they were at a dead end with regards to tracing the text back to the sender.

The director finally called a wrap on the day's shooting just after eight that night. It took Bria another half hour to get out of her wardrobe and makeup, then they drove back to her townhouse on the Upper West Side.

West had secured several parking spaces in the garage across from Bria's townhouse and gotten permission, via a hefty fee, to install cameras so that the spaces could be monitored from the West offices at all times. It was the best they could do for the moment, since Bria continued to refuse to go to a safe house.

Xavier scanned the street as he hustled Bria toward her townhouse, wishing she'd agreed to stay somewhere that at least had an attached garage. They made it to the sidewalk in front of Bria's home when he noticed movement several yards ahead of them. A man huddled behind one of the lampposts that lined the sidewalk. The man's head popped out from behind the post, and the light from the yellow bulb overhead glinted off something in the man's hand.

Xavier propelled Bria through the gate surrounding her property. "Go inside and lock the door. Don't open it for anyone."

He didn't wait to see if she followed his direction before he took off down the sidewalk.

The man looked around the post again, his eyes going wide. He turned, darted between two cars parked at the curb and then dashed across the street.

Xavier caught him by the collar as he made it onto the opposite sidewalk and slammed him face forward against the side of a parked SUV.

"Who are you?" Xavier barked.

"What the hell!" the man stammered, trying to wrench himself out of Xavier's grasp.

Holding him in place with one hand, Xavier patted him down, ripping the man's wallet from his back pocket.

His California driver's license gave his name as Bernard Steele and listed an address in Los Angeles.

"Let me go! I'm going to call the cops," Bernard wailed.

"What are you doing here skulking on this street?"

"Hey, man. It's a free country!"

Xavier gave the man a shake. "Do you feel free right now?" he growled into the man's ear.

The click of fast-moving footsteps had both men turning their heads.

Bria appeared around the side of the SUV Xavier held Steele against.

"I told you to go inside and lock the door," Xavier barked, frustration lining his voice. "Stay back."

"Bria, get this jerk off of me," Steele stuttered.

Xavier pressed the man against the car a little harder.

"Xavier, he's not here to hurt me. Bernie is a photographer. Part of the paparazzi, to be exact."

Xavier hesitated before taking a step back and allowing Bernie to turn to face him.

"Paparazzi?" No one was supposed to know that Bria owned a home on this block. He was sure they hadn't been followed from the set when he'd driven her here, so how did the photographer know where to wait for Bria?

"Your man is crazy!" Steele glared at Bria. "He broke my camera."

Xavier scanned the asphalt. A black digital camera lay on its side next to the SUV's tire.

"I'm going to sue the hell out of you, Brianna Baker."

Xavier bent, picking up the camera. The screen was black and had a spiderweb of cracks running through it now.

Bria stepped closer and Xavier angled his body so that he was between her and Steele.

She frowned at him before turning her attention back to the photographer. "Let's just everyone calm down. My bodyguard may have overreacted a bit, but you were lurking, and there was no way to know you weren't actually a threat. How about I buy you a new camera and we can forget about this whole misunderstanding."

"Misunderstanding," Steele sputtered. "He assaulted me. I'm calling the cops."

Bria fisted a hand on her hip. "And how many times have you pushed and bumped and prodded me, trying to get that million-dollar picture? Maybe I should start calling the cops. As a matter of fact, I'm pretty sure New York has laws against stalking. Surely hiding in the trees outside someone's home in order to get a photo of them qualifies."

"I wasn't hiding in the trees or stalking you," Steele said unconvincingly.

Bria tilted her head and gave a saccharine smile. "Oh no? Well, that's how I'm going to tell the story. And we all know how convincingly I can tell a story, don't we, Bernie?"

Steele swore under his breath. "A new camera to-morrow."

"Tomorrow," Bria agreed.

"Fine," Steele acquiesced, taking a small step forward and finding Xavier blocking his getaway.

"Do you mind," Bernie spat, gesturing for Xavier to step back.

Xavier didn't move.

"Xavier," Bria said, exasperated.

"I have some questions for this guy, first." Now that he was more or less certain that Steele wasn't a real threat to Bria, he shifted so that he was at her back and she was less exposed to anyone else who might come along. He'd have liked to take his interrogation of the photographer inside, but having this man in Bria's house wasn't happening.

"What questions?" Steele crossed his arms over his chest.

"How did you know to wait for Bria on this street?"

Steele scoffed. "I'm not telling you that."

Xavier took a menacing step forward and was gratified to see fear leap into Steele's eyes.

"Xavier." Bria rested a hand on his bicep and a tantalizing heat flushed through his body despite the circumstances. "Bernie, I could still call the cops."

Steele let out a pained sigh. "Look, I can't go burning my sources. They'll stop talking to me if I do."

"Give me a break," Bria laughed. "You're not exactly Bob Woodward breaking Watergate. You sneak up on celebrities to catch them in an awkward photo."

"Way to minimize my life's work." Steele sniffed. "Really makes me want to help you guys."

"Steele!" Xavier bellowed. "You're testing my patience here." He leaned closer, crowding into the man's personal space.

Steele held his hands up in a surrender pose. "Okay, whatever, it's not even worth it. I got an anonymous tip. A call from a burner phone, saying Bria had a place on this block. I've been scoping it out for a few hours now. I was almost ready to give up when I saw you guys heading for the house."

Xavier held his hand out. "Let me see your phone."

Steele must have realized it wasn't a request.

He took his cell from his jacket pocket and slapped it into Xavier's hand. "The call came in earlier today. Around noon."

Xavier scrolled through the list until he got to the blocked number. There wasn't a lot of information to be had other than the time the call had come in and the length of the message, but he noted that the number was the same as the one that had accompanied the photo and threat against him to Bria earlier in the day. So their guy knew where Bria lived. Not good. He had to talk her into staying at a safe house whether she liked it or not. In the meantime, Steele might be their best lead when it came to finding the stalker.

"Was the caller a man or a woman?" Xavier asked Steele.

Steele shook his head. "Couldn't tell. It sounded like they were using one of those digital voice-changing apps or something."

Another dead end. Xavier fought against frustration. "Do you usually believe tips from random, anonymous callers?"

"Man, I get tips from all kinds of people. You wouldn't believe it. This one seemed like it might be credible. I knew Bria was filming in the city and she is from New York, so it seemed plausible she had a secret love shack somewhere in town." Bernie smirked.

Xavier itched to smack the smirk off the man's face, but that was likely to end the cooperation he was currently getting. "Notice anything unusual about the call? Background noise? A car horn? Anything?"

"Nah, man. It was a short call. The person gave me an address for Bria and said she was staying there while she was filming. Then they hung up."

A gust of wind blew down the street and Bria shivered next to him. He needed to wrap this up and get her inside where it was not only warm but safer than standing out in the open.

"Have you been taking photos on the movie set?"

"Not on set, because I haven't found a way in. Yet," Steele said, obviously put out about that fact. Given the pathetic nature of the building's security,

Xavier could only surmise that Bernie was lazy or bad at his job. "But I have gotten some good shots from hanging just outside the perimeter."

"Have you noticed anyone suspicious lurking around or asking about Bria?"

Steele grinned. "Man, there's always someone asking about Brianna. She's Princess Kaleva. Hollywood's It Girl of the moment."

The man was working on Xavier's last nerve, but he gathered what was left of his patience and tried again. "Anyone who struck you as a little too much of a fan? Maybe a little bit obsessed."

Steele cocked his head, thinking about the question. "Not really."

"No or not really?" Xavier growled.

Steele held his hands out in surrender pose. "No, okay, I mean there are just the usual lookie-loos, fans and whatever, you know."

Xavier held his frustration in check. Taking a step forward, he made sure to crowd into Steele's personal space again. "It's in your best interest to keep Bria's address to yourself. And I'm only going to tell you this once. If I catch you hanging around here again, you won't have to worry about calling the cops, understand?"

Steele tried for an unaffected stare, but Xavier was good at reading people. The man was scared. Good.

After a moment, Steele looked at Bria. "I better get that camera tomorrow."

"I said you would and you will," Bria shot back. "I'll have it sent to your office first thing."

Xavier handed over the broken camera but not before taking out the memory card.

"Hey!" Steele exclaimed.

"I'll hold on to this to help keep you honest," Xavier said. There wasn't much he could do if Steele had already backed up the photos and videos he'd taken of Bria to the cloud, but at least he'd have the originals. Maybe he'd caught something that could help them find the stalker, even if he didn't realize it.

"That wasn't part of the deal," Steele grumbled.

"It is now," Xavier barked back.

Bria gave Steele a what-can-you-do shrug and a movie star smile. "You'll have your new camera tomorrow, Bernie. The best model on the market." Bria held up three fingers in the Girl Scout salute. "I promise."

Steele took his broken camera and shot another glare at Xavier before stepping away.

"Bernie," Xavier called out, stopping the paparazzo before he got far. "Remember what I said, Steele. If I see you on this street again, I won't be nearly as friendly."

Chapter Eleven

Once they'd gotten inside and were safe behind a locked door and the alarm system, Xavier read her the riot act for not following his earlier instructions. Or what amounted to the riot act for him, which meant bluntly telling her how stupid it was not to have thought about her safety first. Then he'd started pressing again to take her to a safe house. She was too exhausted to argue with him, so she didn't. Instead, she shot off an email to her assistant about purchasing a camera for Bernie and grabbed a wine cooler and the leftover risotto from the fridge and took it to her room to eat alone and in peace.

The texted threat against Xavier had rattled her to her core. Xavier had always made her feel safe. He was the epitome of the strong, protective type, but the threat against him reminded her that he could be hurt just like anyone else. Tonight it had only been Bernie lurking in the shadows, but what if some night soon it was someone far more dangerous? She couldn't handle it if Xavier was hurt because of her.

Tomorrow she was going to tell Ryan West she wanted a different bodyguard. Or better yet, she'd fire West Investigations altogether. Ryan was right, there were other security firms just as good as West Investigations. Security firms that didn't employ the man whom she had feelings for. Feelings she knew had grown deeper in the years they'd been apart.

And then she wouldn't have to tell Xavier what she'd done during the *Murder in Cabin Nine* filming and watch as he realized the kind of person she was. She knew the photo of her and Derek was the stalker's way of telling her he knew her secret. But how? She'd never told anyone. It was her deepest, darkest secret. Did the stalker intend to expose her? Or was it a prelude to blackmail? She spent hours in her bedroom, her mind shifting between concern for Xavier's safety and fear that her terrible secret was on the verge of being publicly exposed.

She wasn't sure when she fell asleep. It felt as if she'd only been dozing for a moment when a loud noise jolted Bria awake. Her bedside clock read 3:58 a.m. She sat up in bed and the sound came again. A thud against the front door.

She climbed out of bed and went to the window, careful to stay to the side, even though she knew she couldn't be seen from outside. She peeked out.

She caught sight of the tail end of a black sedan before it sped out of sight. An Uber dropping someone off, maybe? But she didn't see anyone making their way to any of the neighboring houses. She scanned the street until her gaze fell on what looked to be a bundle of clothes lying in front of the black iron gate surrounding her front lawn.

Her heart hitched at the sudden realization that what she was looking at wasn't a bundle of clothes at all. It was a person and they appeared to be hurt.

A knock sounded at her bedroom door and she pulled it open to find Xavier standing on the other side. He wore his pajama bottoms and a wrinkled white T-shirt. In his hand was a menacing-looking black gun.

"Are you okay?" he asked, his gaze panning past her to scan the room.

"Yes. But I think there's someone outside who needs help." She waved him to the window and they both looked out together.

Xavier cursed. "Stay here. Lock the door and don't open it to anyone but me."

He glided down the stairs. She turned back into the room and grabbed her robe from the foot of her bed, shrugging into it before following him down the stairs.

He had the front door open and was making his way down the steps carefully, toward the person lying on the sidewalk in front of her home.

Xavier knelt next to the body of a man, feeling for a pulse.

She hurried to his side, then mentally kicked herself when she realized her phone was still in the house charging on her bedside table. A moment later, shock gripped her as she focused in on the face of the man lying in front of her, realization setting in.

Bernie Steele.

They'd just spoken to him only hours ago and now he was… She wouldn't let herself think what her eyes were telling her.

"I'll go back in and call an ambulance," she said, making a move to turn back to the house.

"Ask for the police." Xavier pulled his hand away from Bernie's neck and looked up at her from his crouched position. "He doesn't need an ambulance. He's dead."

Chapter Twelve

The street outside Bria's home swarmed with police and emergency services vehicles. The first officer to arrive on scene had separated him from Bria and now they were each being questioned by detectives separately. Thankfully, they'd deferred to Bria's celebrity, and the implied threat of a host of lawyers keeping them from their two best witnesses, and consented to doing their questioning in Bria's house. Bria was in the living room being questioned and he sat at the kitchen counter with Detective Oliver Roslak. Roslak had a mop of brown hair and wore a wrinkled black suit over an equally wrinkled blue shirt. Despite his slightly disheveled appearance, his gaze was sharp and intelligent.

"Okay, walk me through it again, if you don't mind," Detective Roslak said, casually looking down at his notebook.

"No."

Roslak looked up, startled by his matter-of-fact refusal.

He had already walked Roslak through everything that had happened from the time he and Bria returned to her house until the moment the first officers arrived. Roslak had tried to act nonchalant, but he knew enough about police work to realize that he'd be a suspect, at least for a while, given the encounter he'd had with Bernie right before his death. Bria and the security system in the townhouse would provide him an alibi of sorts, but he was a security specialist. He knew there wasn't a system in existence that couldn't be manipulated, and given his past and maybe current relationship with Bria, he wasn't sure how inclined the detectives would be to believe her.

Nope. He'd told his story and he wasn't going to give the man the opportunity to twist his words.

Roslak forced a smile, but his eyes were narrowed to slits. The combined effect made him look like a lizard. "This is just routine questioning. I just need to make sure I got the details right."

"I'm sure you do, Detective. But I'm not going to sit here and go through rounds and rounds of questioning. I told you what transpired tonight. We'll make the home's security information available to you and your medical examiner will tell you that Bernie was dead before his body hit the sidewalk. That should be enough to clear Miss Baker and myself."

"You think?" Roslak growled.

Xavier just smiled.

"Mr. Nichols, this is a serious matter. Now, I'm sure you don't want it to get out that you're not co-operating with a homicide investigation."

He folded his hands on his lap. "I'm sure I don't care. I've told you what I know."

Roslak slammed his notebook closed. "Okay, I'll tell you what I know. By your own admission, you and the victim got into a heated argument last night in which you put your hands on him. That's assault. I could arrest you for that right now."

Xavier held his wrists out. "Do it. You and I both know the charges won't stick, and after I've been charged, you won't be able to talk to me without counsel present. No lawyer worth their salt will let their client talk to the cops after a charge has been laid against them. And trust me, my lawyer will be worth his salt."

Brandon West, Ryan and Shawn's older brother, was a top-notch attorney, as was Shawn's wife, Addy. Both lawyers were used to swooping in and getting West Investigations' employees out of stickier jams that the one Roslak was proposing. They'd both probably read him the riot act for talking to Roslak without one of them present now, but he had nothing to hide, despite Roslak's unabashed suspicion.

Roslak swore. "Let me pose a hypothetical for you, then. You don't have to talk since you're so shy," he said with a derisive snort. "You and the victim got into it earlier in the evening. You're enraged because he's been following you. You rough him up a little bit and tell him to get lost, but he doesn't do that. You find him poking around later that night. Maybe he's even peeping in the windows, catching a glimpse of you and the woman playing slap and tickle."

Xavier clenched his fists and reminded himself that Roslak was trying to get a rise out of him. An arrest for assault when the propertied victim couldn't press charges would be thrown out in a heartbeat. But an arrest for assaulting a police detective would be much harder to make disappear.

"Or maybe he's just peeping on her," Roslak added, after taking a beat to see if his goading was working. "I hear nudie pics of the right celebrity can bring in real money."

"I wouldn't know," Xavier shot back. "You clearly hang out with a lower-brow crowd than I do."

Roslak scowled and continued. "You lash out at the victim. Stab him, and realizing that now you have to do something with the body, make up this ridiculous story about finding him on the front stoop."

"On the sidewalk in front of the house. And the only thing ridiculous here is your story. Bria allowed you to search the house. You didn't find a knife. There's no blood anywhere in or around the house, including out on the sidewalk where the body was found, which confirms that the murder happened elsewhere. Your hypothetical doesn't match up with the facts, Detective."

Roslak huffed but didn't say anything more.

"So, are we through here?" Xavier stood.

"For the moment." Roslak rose. "Stay available, Mr. Nichols."

"Always, Detective Roslak."

BERNIE WAS DEAD. From the snatch of conversation she'd overheard between the paramedics, who had arrived shortly after she'd called, he was dead before he landed on the sidewalk in front of her townhouse. He'd been stabbed in the chest, then transported to her front door.

A shudder snaked through her.

"Take me over the events of the evening one more time." Detective Ivy Morris held her pen poised over the small notebook in her hands. She crossed her thin brown legs at the ankle. Her boxy suit was ill fitting but didn't hide the curvy figure beneath.

Bria massaged her temples. "Do I have to? I already told you everything I know, which isn't much."

Detective Morris smiled sympathetically. "I know it's been a long night. Just one more time so I know I have everything straight in my head."

Bria sighed heavily and leaned against the arm of the sofa she was sitting on. Morris's partner was taking Xavier's statement in the kitchen. Bria glanced toward the back of the house, but she wasn't able to make out Xavier or the detective.

"Something, a sound, woke me up just before four this morning. I didn't know exactly what it was, but it happened again and it sounded like it was coming from outside."

"Did you have any idea what the noise was?" Detective Morris asked.

Bria shook her head. "No. It just sounded like a thud. Maybe like someone falling, but I can't be sure."

"It appears that someone threw two rocks at your front door. We found them on the porch and there's a bit of damage to the door."

Bria pressed her palms together. She hadn't noticed any rocks, but she took the woman at her word. So someone wanted to make sure that she and Xavier were the ones to find Bernie's body and not some passerby. And Bria was sure that someone was her stalker.

"Can you tell me what happened next?" Detective Morris prodded.

"I got out of the bed and peered through the window. I saw something that looked like a pile of clothes on the sidewalk in front of my house." She continued retelling the events of the night.

Detective Morris scratched out notes and nodded for her to go on.

"There was a knock on the bedroom door and Xavier asked if I was okay. I took him to the window to show him what was outside. He told me to stay inside, but I followed him out of the front door." She took a steadying breath for what came next. "I didn't realize it was Bernie at first, but I could see that it was a person, a man. I'd left my phone in the house, so I started to turn back to go call for an ambulance when I realized I knew the person in front of me."

"And by Bernie you are referring to Bernard Steele?" Morris scribbled notes.

Bria nodded. "Yes."

"And you knew him, how?"

"He's a paparazzo. He's followed me for years now, taking my picture."

"You live in Los Angeles, correct?" Detective Morris looked at her with more than a hint of suspicion. "He followed you all the way across the country for a picture?"

"Celebrity photographs are big business, Detective. The paparazzi will follow an actor or actress all over the world for the chance to get a million-dollar photo."

The woman looked at her with open skepticism. "Million dollar?"

"It's a figure of speech, but the right shot can sell for anywhere from one thousand to ten thousand dollars. Or more, if the photo is an exclusive."

Morris let out a low whistle. "That's a lot for a picture."

"Exactly. Bernie has made taking my photo a significant part of his business model."

"So you knew him well?" Morris was back to scribbling in her notebook.

"Knew him? Not really. We weren't friends. He wasn't the worst of the paparazzi though."

"I understand there was an argument between Mr. Nichols and the victim earlier in the evening." Morris kept her tone light, but Bria got the hint.

"I wouldn't describe it as an argument. Xavier was escorting me home when he spotted someone he believed might be a threat. He approached and we discovered it was Bernie. Xavier asked him some questions and then advised him not to loiter on the street in front of my home."

Detective Morris's brow went up. "That's not how one of your neighbors described it. They heard the victim yelling about a camera, that he'd been assaulted and threatening to call the police."

Bria shrugged. "Bernie dropped his camera. He was upset, and not unexpectedly given his line of work, he tends…tended—" she corrected herself "—toward the dramatic. I offered to buy him a new camera and he calmed down." Bria guessed she'd have to cancel that order now.

"That's a very different story than the one your neighbor told us."

She shrugged. "I don't know what my neighbor told you, but I was standing right there. That's what happened." Or close enough. There was no way she was going to give Detective Morris grounds to suspect Xavier any more than she already did. Her version of events was close enough since there was no way that Xavier had anything to do with Bernie's murder. She'd told her about the text message threatening Xavier, and about the other emails, notes and flowers she'd received from her stalker. Detective Morris had listened but didn't appear to be putting much stock into the idea that her stalker had progressed to murder, much to Bria's chagrin. It was obvious who could have killed Bernie, but Morris was far more interested in the confrontation between Xavier and Bernie than she was in hearing about the stalker.

"Okay, so after the…discussion between Mr. Nichols and Mr. Steele, what happened?"

"Nothing. Bernie drove off and Xavier and I went into my house."

She eyed her warily. "And then…"

"It was late and I was exhausted. I went up to bed."

"By yourself?"

Her face heated further. "Xavier is staying in the guest room if that's what you're asking."

Detective Morris gave an apologetic smile. "I'm not trying to pry into your personal life. I'm just trying to ascertain whether the two of you were together for the whole evening."

"I went upstairs to my room and he went up to his a few minutes after me."

"And about what time did you go to sleep?"

"I'm not sure exactly. I went to my room around nine fifteen, but I didn't go to sleep right away."

"So you can't vouch for Mr. Nichols's whereabouts after you went to bed at 9:15 p.m. Is that correct?"

Bria's back straightened. "Xavier didn't kill Bernie."

Detective Morris pressed her lips together tightly. "Ms. Baker, after 9:15 p.m., you can't say exactly where Mr. Nichols was, correct?"

Bria ignored the question for a second time. "Xavier didn't do this. He doesn't have a motive, but more importantly, if he'd left the house the alarm would have sounded."

"He's been staying here, but he doesn't know the alarm code?" Morris shot back.

"He does, of course," Bria gritted out. "But when the alarm is deactivated, even with the code, it beeps. It would have woken me, I'm sure of it."

Detective Morris didn't look convinced. She wrote something in her notebook. "Is there anything else you can tell me?"

"Would you listen if I did?" Bria said.

The detective closed her notebook. "Ms. Baker, I'm just trying to do my job here. A man has been killed and I intend to find out who did it."

Footsteps approached from the hall. Xavier and Roslak appeared.

"I've finished taking Mr. Nichols's statement," Roslak said.

Detective Morris rose. "And I've just finished up with Ms. Baker." Roslak looked from Bria to Xavier.

"Neither of you have any plans to leave town in the near future, do you?"

"I'm shooting a movie here for the next month," Bria responded. "And I'm pretty hard to lose track of. Just open any tabloid and there I am."

"I've no plans to leave town at the moment," Xavier answered far less sarcastically.

"Good. Good. Well, then we will be in touch."

Bria walked the detectives to the foyer. With the door open, she could see the ambulance and most of the police cruisers had left while she'd been giving her statement. The street was almost back to normal except for the unmarked sedan double-parked a few feet from her home. Still, she couldn't help but see Bernie's lifeless body lying on the pavement.

She closed the door quickly and turned, pulling up short when she found Xavier waiting only inches away.

"We need to talk," he said.

Bria stifled a groan. "Xavier, I'm really not up for it."

She moved to go past him, but he stepped in front of her.

"Too bad. It's no longer safe for you to stay here. Bernie knew you owned this place and apparently so did whoever killed him. And I'm sure that in a matter of hours, so will the entirety of the New York paparazzi, if they don't already."

This time she didn't try to stifle the groan that escaped from her lips.

He placed his hands on her shoulders. "More importantly, it's time for you to tell me everything."

"What are you talking about?"

"This secret of yours that the stalker thinks he knows. And the photo of you and your former costar. What is going on, Bria? Do you know who's stalking you?"

Chapter Thirteen

"Of course not." Bria stalked past him into the kitchen.

"Then, what are you keeping from me?" Xavier followed her.

She programmed the coffee maker and contemplated how loaded his question was. A lot had happened in the fifteen years since she'd broken up with him, but she knew that wasn't what he was asking.

He wanted to know about the photo of her and Derek Longwell. Why the stalker had left it for her.

She couldn't be sure, but she had a good hunch. And if she was right, if her stalker knew her deepest, darkest secret, her career was over. And most likely her freedom as well. But she also knew that Xavier wouldn't give up. He'd keep asking until he wore her down or he'd go out and investigate himself. And that, she didn't want.

If he had to know her secret, she wanted to be the one to tell him. Even if it meant he'd never see her the same way again. She took her mug from the coffee dispenser and carried it to the island.

Xavier hopped onto the stool next to her.

Bria wrapped her hands around the mug, soaking in its warmth and taking a sip to fortify herself before she said the words that could change her life forever. "Derek Longwell was the star of a C-list indie film that I got cast in about three years after I'd moved to Los Angeles. The budget wasn't big, but we all had visions of the film becoming a breakout indie hit like *The Blair Witch Project* and other indie films around that time period." She gripped the sides of her coffee mug. "The entire cast and crew was young and mostly just happy to have a paying job on a real movie."

"What happened?"

Bria slowly let out a deep breath. "I killed Derek Longwell."

Xavier looked at her impassively. "Start at the beginning."

Bria's hands shook just going back to that night in her memory. "The film's shoot was scheduled to take a little over a month. We were about two weeks, maybe a little more into it and shooting was going well. The cast and crew would often hang out at a bar about a few blocks from the motel where we were staying. Most of us were at the bar one night, celebrating after having spent two days shooting a pivotal scene. There was lots of drinking. Some drugs, although I never partook in that. The rest of the cast and crew was still going strong around midnight, but I was ready to call it a night, so I headed out to walk back to the motel. It wasn't far."

The trembling in her hands became more pronounced. She'd never told anyone what had happened that night, for good reason, but somehow telling Xavier was harder than she'd ever imagined. It wasn't just that telling him her secret could be the end of the career, the life, she'd worked so hard to build. It mattered to her that he believed her, and the possibility that he might not, that he might turn against her, was more terrifying than any of the other possible consequences of her confession.

He reached out and took her hand, the simple gesture giving her enough hope to continue telling her story.

"I didn't make it out of the parking lot before Derek caught up to me. He said it wouldn't be right to let me walk home alone at night. There was a path through a wooded area that you had to use to get back to the motel, so I was more than happy to have company. He was drunk, a little unsteady on his feet, but I'd seen him in much worse conditions since we'd started filming. We were on the path when he suddenly grabbed me and kissed me. I pushed him away, tried to make light of it but also let him know that I wasn't interested. But he didn't care what I wanted. He grabbed me again, pulled me into the trees and his hands were all over me. I fought back, but he hit me."

His grip on her hand tightened, not to the point of hurting her, but she could tell by the hard set of his jaw and the fire in his eyes that he was teetering on the edge of rage.

"I fell and he was on top of me." The memory slammed into her. She took a steadying breath before continuing. "I knew he wasn't going to stop, and as hard as I was fighting him, he was much stronger than I was. I don't even remember picking up the rock, but it was in my hands and I smashed it against the side of Derek's head. He screamed and rolled off of me. I didn't wait around to see if he needed help, I just got up and ran back to my room at the motel."

"You didn't call the police? Report his assault?" His words were little more than a growl, but she knew the anger wasn't directed at her. She could hear the pain in them.

Bria shook her head, the terror of that night as real at that moment as it had been twelve years earlier. "I think I was in shock or something. Derek was the star—" she made air quotes "—of the movie. His stepfather had put up most of the money that was being used to produce the film. Even if the director and crew believed me, their jobs were dependent on Derek, not me. I was expendable."

"You have never been expendable," Xavier said fiercely.

"I spent the whole night huddled in my room, waiting for Derek to break down the door and try to finish what he'd started or for the police to come and arrest me for assaulting him."

"But neither happened."

She shook her head. "No. The next morning everyone returned to set. Everyone except Derek. It wasn't unusual for him to be late, so no one was worried at first. I just tried to act like everything was normal. Like nothing had happened. I hoped Derek would be embarrassed enough by his behavior that he'd just make up some story about the injury to his head and let it go." She shuddered out a breath. "Eventually, we got word that a couple on an early morning hike had found Derek's body. I was terrified and sure that I was going to jail."

"Did the police question you?" Xavier asked softly, and although she could still hear the fury in the words, he seemed to have wrested it under control.

She nodded. "They questioned all of us. Maybe I should have told them the truth, but I was still a nobody then. Derek's stepfather was some bigwig hedge fund or investment banker or something. He had connections. I didn't know what he'd do to protect his stepson, even in death."

"The truth is Derek Longwell was a creep who assaulted you and you defended yourself. The truth is his death was an accident brought on by his own actions."

How many people were in jail who had told the truth believing the system would work? "I told the cops that Derek had walked me back to my room and said he was going to go back to the bar. He was drunk, everyone at the bar could attest to that. I don't think the police in that town had the wherewithal to conduct a real investigation. A few days later, they officially ruled Derek's death an accident. It was March, but we were in a densely wooded area and the temperature at night was consistently in the thirties or lower. They concluded he was drunk, fell and hit his head. I think the official ruling was a combination of blood loss and hypothermia from the cold. I've carried the guilt with me ever since."

"You have nothing to feel guilty about."

She wished she could believe him. "I could have called for help. Sent someone to check on him."

"You said it yourself. You were in shock. You'd just been victimized yourself and you weren't sure that summoning help was going to do anything other than open you up to further trauma. Your actions are understandable."

Bria rose and stalked across the kitchen, putting her now-empty mug in the sink. "My actions might be the reason the stalker is terrorizing me now."

"I will find whoever is doing this."

Bria kept her back to Xavier, her hands gripping the countertop on either side of the sink. So many thoughts had swirled in her head since finding that photo with the flowers, but there was one she just couldn't seem to shake no matter how ludicrous it seemed.

She turned to face Xavier, still using her hands to brace herself against the countertop. "I've been thinking that maybe, I don't know how, but maybe Derek is the one doing this."

Xavier cocked an eyebrow. "Maybe he isn't really dead?"

"I'm not sure, but no one else was aware what happened that night."

"We aren't certain that anyone does know about Derek's assault on you."

Bria shot him an incredulous look. "What other possible message could the stalker mean to convey by that photo and all the references to 'my secret'? Hitting Derek and not owning up to the truth of that is by far the worst thing I've ever done. Maybe—" She paused, swallowing hard before forcing the next words out of her mouth. "Maybe I should go to the police and confess everything? Then the stalker wouldn't have anything to hold over me and he wouldn't have any reason to go after you."

Her resolve to fire West Investigations to keep Xavier out of harm's way had faltered with the light of day and finding Bernie's body. She wanted Xavier safe, but she wanted him at her side too.

Xavier rose and crossed the tile floor. He cupped her face in his hands. "I can take care of myself. Confessing to a crime you didn't commit isn't going to get this guy to stop. That's not how stalkers operate. We are going to figure this out. The photo, the stalking, everything, but you have to trust me. Can you do that?"

She let go of the countertop and wove her hands around his waist, keeping her eyes trained on his. "The answer to that is easy. I already trust you. I always have."

Chapter Fourteen

Xavier stalked into the West Investigations head-quarters. His emotions were still in upheaval from Bria's revelation. She'd been attacked and may have killed a man.

And I wasn't there to protect her.

He knew it was a waste of time to blame himself for something he had no control over, but he couldn't seem to stop himself. Bria thought she'd taken a life and he knew firsthand how that weighed on a person. He'd had no choice, that someone was likely to die at your hand was a fact of life for a soldier at war, but that didn't mean he felt the significance of that act any less acutely. He often felt it was the exact opposite.

He should have been there, but he was here now. And he would move heaven and earth to protect her.

Bria wasn't on the shooting schedule for the next two days and he needed to talk to Ryan about their next steps in person. He'd enlisted another West Investigations employee, Gideon Wright, to stay with Bria while he was at West headquarters.

Ryan was in his office. He waved Xavier into a chair in front of his desk and set the report he'd been reading aside.

"Xavier, I'm glad you're here. Seems you had one hell of a morning."

He'd called Ryan before the police arrived at Bria's house and had given him a quick heads-up on having found the paparazzo's body in front of Bria's townhouse. Now he gave a more fulsome description of the morning's events.

"I don't like this one bit," Ryan said. "This is a huge escalation if the stalker is our killer."

"It is, and we know that Bria's stalker is motivated. He followed her across the country."

"And we know that a changed situation can push a stalker to act out." Ryan jutted his chin in Xavier's direction. "You're a new element in Bria's life and he issued a threat to you with that text message. It's possible that he saw the photographer as a threat too."

"And it would be a whole lot easier to get to him than it would be to get to me."

"Exactly," Ryan agreed. "If this guy wants to show Bria just how serious he is about making her his, killing a man who is, for all intents and purposes, also stalking Bria is one way to do it."

Xavier drew in a breath. "There's more I need to tell you."

Ryan shot him a weary look but gestured for him to go on. Xavier recounted what Bria told him about the night Derek Longwell attacked her.

As Ryan listened, his expression reflected increasing concern. "So Bria's stalker could be connected somehow to this actor Derek Longwell's death."

"It's possible," Xavier conceded.

"You know this information makes West's association with Bria much more complicated. She confessed to killing a man."

Xavier felt his body tense. "It was self-defense."

"I'm not saying it wasn't, but it doesn't change the fact that a man is dead and Bria didn't tell the authorities the whole truth concerning the incident," Ryan shot back.

"We're not turning her in."

Ryan sighed. "I have to think about this firm."

"Fine. I quit." Xavier stood. "I'll handle Bria's security myself, and if you go to the authorities, I'll deny I told you anything."

"Just slow down." Ryan held up his hands. "I'm not going to the police." The unspoken *yet* hung in the air between them. "I suggest we look into Derek Longwell's life and death ourselves. See if we can't pinpoint our stalker and maybe drum up some evidence that might support Bria's claim of self-defense."

Xavier held his hands fisted at his sides. "I'm never going to agree to turn her in to the cops."

"I gathered that. But it might not be up to you. If

her stalker really does know about what she did to Longwell, he could reveal it at any time. It will be better for Bria if we're already prepared when and if that happens."

Xavier hesitated for a moment before giving a terse nod. Everything Ryan said made sense even if he didn't like it.

"I need to talk to Bria. Without you in the room," Ryan said.

"Why? I've already told you what she said."

Ryan gave him a hard look. "You are too close to this situation. You don't just want to protect Bria, you want to save her and that's clouding your ability to be objective."

"I can be objective," he growled.

Ryan snorted.

"Fine, I'm not objective. I'm breaking the cardinal rule of private protection. I have feelings for the woman I'm supposed to be protecting. But you ought to know better than anyone how that feels. How it can make you crazy but also sharpen your instincts because you have something to lose if you make the wrong decision."

It was well-known among those who worked for West Security and Investigations that Ryan's wife Nadia was a client when the two of them met and fell in love. Nadia's brother had gotten himself, and by extension her, into a heap of trouble with organized crime. Ryan had thrown every resource West had at protecting Nadia and helping her out of the jam her brother had created, despite warnings from his brother Shawn and several other people.

Ryan held his hands up in surrender. "Fine. I'm a hypocrite. I'd do… I did the same thing you're doing. But that's how I know it can go disastrously bad. I did end up in the hospital and Nadia was kidnapped."

"I remember you were fine and you saved Nadia's life. All I'm asking is the chance to do the same for the woman I…" Xavier caught himself before he said what he'd been thinking. What he'd been feeling since he'd walked into the conference room days earlier and seen Bria sitting there. Hell, if he was honest, it was what he'd felt since the moment he saw her sitting on that park bench in Bryant Park fifteen years earlier.

He loved her. He'd never stopped loving her despite her having given him the heave-ho fourteen years ago.

"The woman you what?" Ryan said, his mouth upturning ever so slightly.

He was sure Ryan knew what he'd been about to say, but he wasn't ready to profess his love for Bria to Ryan out loud. "The woman I've been charged with protecting."

Ryan shook his head. "You've got your head so far up your…" he mumbled, letting the thought trail off. "Look, I'll concede that, despite your emotional involvement, you are the best person to watch over

Bria. But I need you to trust me. I need to talk to Bria if West Investigations is going to help her."

I need you to trust me. Hadn't he asked the same of Bria only hours earlier? He did trust Ryan. He'd trusted Ryan, Shawn, Gideon and all of the other operatives at West literally with his life on more than one occasion, but somehow it was harder to trust them with Bria's life.

Because she means more to you than your life does, the voice inside his head intoned.

And that was the heart of it. He'd willingly give his own life for Bria's, but of course, he couldn't expect the same of anyone else at West Investigations. Still, despite his earlier threat to quit and protect her alone, he knew that having Ryan and the West team on his side was the best chance they had of figuring out the connection between Derek Longwell's death and Bria's stalker.

"Fine."

"Good." Ryan was all business. "Gideon's with her now?"

Xavier nodded.

"I'll have him bring her into the office. While I speak to her, you should pull everything you can find on Derek Longwell and the *Murder in Cabin Nine* movie."

"Bria said the film was shelved after Derek's death. His stepfather was one of the major funders and apparently after Derek was gone, he didn't see any reason to continue financing the venture."

"Still, at the very least we need to try to dig up a list of the cast and crew of the film. Occam's razor. The most obvious answer to the identity of our stalker is that he or she worked on *Murder in Cabin Nine* or was close to someone who worked on the movie. If nothing else, it's the logical place to start given the photograph that was left with the flowers in Bria's trailer."

"I'll get started on that." Xavier rose and headed for the door.

"Xavier." Ryan's voice stopped him before he left the office.

Xavier turned back to face his boss and friend.

"Be careful. You may be right that your feelings for Bria are an asset now, but they could just as easily turn into a liability. And that could be dangerous for you both."

"I DON'T APPRECIATE being interrogated, especially by people I'm paying to protect me," Bria said, marching into the conference room where Xavier had spread out all the information he and West's researchers had pulled so far on the people closest to Bria. Eliot Sykes. Mika Reynolds. Bria's assistant, Karen Gibbs, who they'd confirmed was still in Los Angeles. They'd also pulled background reports on her costars on *Loss of Days* and her last two films.

The possibilities were quickly becoming over-whelming. Bria literally came into contact with hundreds of people while she was filming a movie and those number swelled into the thousands once they took into account promoting the movies, fans, reporters and any other number of events and award ceremonies she attended in a given year. The stalker could be among these people or completely removed from them. Someone whose connection to Bria was entirely in his or her head, making them virtually impossible to find.

He was currently focusing on the cast and crew from *Murder in Cabin Nine* given the photograph and what Bria had told him, but he really had no way of knowing if he was looking in the right place. *Murder in Cabin Nine* had been a relatively low budget film with a small cast and crew by Hollywood standards, but there were still more than twenty names on the list, including the director and producers.

Xavier rubbed his temples and tried to keep his frustration from bubbling over. "It was necessary. We need to know everything you know."

Bria fell into a chair on the opposite side of the conference room table. "And you didn't believe that I'd told you everything. Is that why you sicced Ryan West on me?"

The vein in his neck jumped. "I didn't sic anyone on you. And I believe you. But Ryan is right. I'm emotionally involved. I'm sure he was better at pressing you, getting you to remember things you didn't even know that you've forgotten, than I would be."

"You didn't trust me to tell you the truth," she said, hurt shining in her eyes.

"I didn't trust me. I didn't trust my feelings for you would let me be as objective as I needed to be to question you properly."

Bria looked away.

Neither of them was happy about the current situation, but deep down, he knew that Ryan was right to have questioned her himself. Now they had to move on and focus on what needed to be done.

"I'd like you to take a look at this list." He pushed the paper indicating the names of the cast and crew of *Murder in Cabin Nine* across the table.

She studied the paper for a moment before looking back up at him. "These are all the people who worked on *Murder in Cabin Nine*."

"Yes. Right now we're working under the theory that the stalker is connected to that film."

Bria shook her head. "I can't imagine anyone I've worked with doing this."

"Someone is, and right now we don't have a lot to go on."

Bria looked at the list again. "Honestly, I can't even remember most of these people." She pointed to one of the names on the paper and smiled. "Rob, I remember though. He was a sweet kid. Everybody's friend."

"Robert Gindry?" Xavier pulled up the information West had compiled so far on Gindry. It wasn't a lot. Gindry wasn't in show business anymore. He'd gotten out of the industry more than ten years before and was now an insurance salesman. And a pretty successful one, based on his address, which Xavier noticed was not that far from Manhattan. "He's not acting anymore and he lives in Connecticut. Just outside of the city."

Bria shook her head. "No way. I know it's been more than ten years since I've spoken a word to him, but Rob was the kindest, sweetest soul you'll ever meet. Everyone loved him. He was everyone's friend. You'll never convince me he's my stalker."

Xavier frowned. That was just the kind of sentiment a lot of predators relied on. Instead, he pressed on. "Anyone else on the list you can tell me something about?"

"The name Morgan Ryder is kind of familiar, but I can't quite grasp why."

He searched for information on Ryder in the files they'd pulled already, but came up empty. "Morgan Ryder. The name is pretty androgynous. Was Ryder male or female?"

Bria shook her head. "I honestly can't remember. I can't pull up a face to go with the name, but there's something about it. It's probably nothing. Maybe he or she is still in the business and we've crossed paths since filming *Murder in Cabin Nine*. Or maybe the name is just reminding me of a character in some script I've read. It could be nothing."

Or it could be something. There was no point in pushing her now though if she couldn't remember. "If you remember what it is, let me know."

"Of course I will."

"There are only two people on this list, that we know of, who live within driving distance. Robert Gindry and Tate Harwood, the director of *Murder in Cabin Nine*."

Bria's brow rose in surprise. "Tate is on the East Coast? I wouldn't have thought he'd ever leave Los Angeles."

"He works for a production company headquartered here in Manhattan. The home address we have for him is in Brooklyn."

"I take it you think we should pay Rob and Tate visits."

"I should pay Gindry and Harwood visits. You should stay safely ensconced in a safe house until your stalker is locked behind bars."

Bria shook her head. "No way. If you go to talk to Rob and Tate, I go with you."

"Bria."

"I'm not some shrinking violet who's just going to cower behind the big strong man while he protects her. And you'll have a much easier time getting Rob and Tate to talk if I'm with you."

"I've never had difficulty getting anyone to talk to me," Xavier growled.

Bria smiled. "I'm sure brute force has its place, but I don't think this is it. Especially when it comes to getting Tate to meet with you. You can't do anything for him, so he's not going to be inclined to give you any of his time."

"And you think he'll talk to you?"

She laughed. "Oh, I know he will."

Chapter Fifteen

The research West Investigations had compiled on Tate Harwood was thorough. His cell phone number was listed among the contact information. It took a moment to convince Tate that the call wasn't a joke or crank call, but just as she'd predicted, once she'd convinced Tate she was who she said she was, he agreed to meet with her. They agreed to a time the next morning and Bria ended the call just as Ryan led Detectives Roslak and Morris into the conference room.

Their arrival seemed to suck all the air out of the room.

Bria glanced from Xavier to Ryan. The two men shared a look, conveying information only the two of them were privy to. What was clear, however, was the tension in both their bodies and the hardness in their expressions.

Detective Roslak stepped in front of Xavier. "We have a few more questions about the night you found Bernard Steele, Mr. Nichols."

"Why don't you and Detective Morris have a seat,

then?" Xavier gestured to the chairs surrounding the conference room table. "I'll be happy to answer whatever questions you have."

Morris's smile was feral. "Actually, we'd like you to answer them down at the station if you don't mind."

Xavier's expression remained unchanged. "And if I do mind?"

"Then we'll have to change this from a request to something more formal," Detective Roslak answered.

Bria took a step closer to Xavier. "Wait a minute—" Her voice came out high-pitched and laced with all the fear for Xavier she felt at that moment. "What the hell is going on here? Xavier didn't even know Bernie."

Ryan laid a hand on her shoulders. "Let's stay calm here. Xavier, you go with the detectives. I'll have Brandon meet you at the station."

Detective Morris glared at Ryan. "An attorney isn't necessary. As we said, we just have a few more questions for Mr. Nichols."

"Let's not be cute, Detective," Xavier growled. "You're not really giving me a choice. Answer your questions voluntarily or you'll arrest me, right?"

Both remained silent.

"I'd say an attorney is most definitely in order," Ryan said.

Bria grasped Xavier's hand and squeezed. "I'm going with you."

She wasn't exactly sure why the detectives wanted

to talk to Xavier, but it was clear from the expressions on his and Ryan's faces that they thought the situation was serious. Whatever was going on, she wanted Xavier to know that he had her support.

He returned her squeeze and gave her a thin smile. "There's no need. Brandon West is one of the best lawyers in the city and there will be nothing for you to do at the police station but wait. Stay here where Ryan can look out for you."

She opened her mouth to object. "Please. It will be easier on me if I know you're safe. And if I'm not back in time to take you, Ryan or someone else from West Investigations can accompany you to your interview this afternoon."

She'd forgotten about the interview. Eliot had sent her the details last night and she'd forwarded it along to Xavier. She was to meet the reporter, Ian Cole, that afternoon at the Ritz Carlton.

She didn't like leaving Xavier to deal with the police alone. Every fiber of her being urged her to stay with him and fight whatever misinformed theory had led the detectives to drag Xavier down to the station. But she trusted him, more and more with each passing day. If he said it was best that she stay here at the West Investigations offices, that's what she'd do.

"Okay," she said reluctantly.

She watched Xavier leave flanked by the two police detectives, more scared in that moment than she'd ever been before.

THE DETECTIVES HAD led Xavier into a small interrogation room when they arrived at the police station and left him there saying they'd be back in a moment. He'd been staring straight ahead, body relaxed, breathing even, for the past half hour. The light on the camera in the upper-left corner was dark, but he knew better than to think that the camera wasn't on and recording. The stark gray cinder block walls of the interrogation room were intended to remind people of the inside of a prison cell, a not-so-subtle intimidation tactic used by the cops in order to get criminals to loosen up. The long absence and drab surroundings no doubt worked to induce most people to talk. He wasn't most people.

The door to the interrogation room finally opened. Brandon West strode in, laying his briefcase on the table before opening it and taking out a leather portfolio. Brandon took the seat next to Xavier while Roslak and Morris slid into the chairs on the opposite side of the table.

"Detectives, does one of you want to tell me why you dragged my client down here to ask him questions you surely could have asked him in a less… coercive environment?" Brandon snapped at them.

"I wouldn't call this a coercive environment for a former decorated soldier such as your client. He's deployed to Iraq and Afghanistan, so I'm sure he's been in much more difficult situations," Detective Morris said in a measured tone.

"I'm sure he has, although I do find your likening this situation to literal war zones interesting." Brandon flashed a smile.

Morris's lips thinned.

Detective Roslak cleared his throat. "As we told your client, there was really no need for you to come to the station, counselor. We just have some routine questions we wanted to ask him."

Brandon leaned forward and pinned Roslak with a look. "You and I both know there is no such thing as routine questions, so let's cut the crap. You ask your questions and I'll decide if my client is going to answer them."

Xavier held back a smirk.

Brandon West may wear five-thousand-dollar suits and spend more on one haircut than Xavier spent all year on shape-ups, but he was a damned good lawyer. Especially, when it came to keeping his brothers and their friends and employees out of the line of police fire. There'd been some talk among the rank and file at West regarding whether they should continue to call on Brandon on the rare occasions they ran afoul of the cops, given that he'd started dating one himself. But it didn't appear that his feelings for Silver Hill detective Yara Thomas had dulled his sharp edges at all. If anything they seemed to have been sharpened to a deadly point.

Roslak and Morris glared back across the table for a long moment before Roslak turned his gaze on Xavier. "Could you go over what happened last night again for us? Starting with your arrival at Ms. Baker's townhome and the confrontation with Bernard Steele."

Brandon tapped one finger against the table, his signal not to answer. "As I understand it, Mr. Nichols has already given you a statement, Detective."

"He has," Roslak gritted out. "We just want to make sure we got everything down correctly."

Brandon's smile was cool. "Why don't you tell us what you're confused about and we'll see if we can help you understand things a little better."

Roslak scowled. "Mr. Nichols, you stated that you had an argument with Mr. Steele. We were able to get the video Mr. Steele took with his camera in front of Ms. Baker's townhome from his online storage, and it seems as if you and Mr. Steele had more than just an argument."

"Is there a question in there somewhere?" Brandon asked in a tone that hinted at boredom.

"Did you put your hands on Mr. Steele?" Detective Morris asked.

Brandon tapped the table once. "If you have the video as you say, you already know the answer to that question."

"I did, and I told you I did in my initial statement," Xavier answered the question, drawing a look of rebuke from Brandon. He appreciated Brandon being here, but it wasn't his style to hide behind a lawyer.

"Yes, well, your statement made it seem as if it was a little skirmish," Morris continued, "but the video shows that it was a bit more than that. You threw the victim against a car, not once but twice and broke his camera, did you not?"

Brandon tapped the table. "Again, a question answered by the video. I don't see why you've brought my client in, detectives."

"We're getting to that, counselor," Roslak growled.

"I pushed Steele against a nearby SUV when I thought he was a danger to the client I was hired to protect. He dropped his camera when I did so. I don't know if it was broken but it couldn't have been too bad if you have video from it."

"Ms. Baker offered to buy Mr. Steele a new camera, did she not?"

"She did," Xavier answered before Brandon could tap.

Brandon sent him another look.

"In fact, Ms. Baker offered the new camera as something of a bribe, correct? To keep Mr. Steele from calling the police and having you arrested for assault."

"He's not answering that question. You're asking my client to speculate on not one but two people's motivations."

"Not a problem." Roslak waved the question off as if it was nothing. "How about this one? Mr. Nichols, you and Ms. Baker aren't just employer and employee or bodyguard and protectee, are you? You've had a long-standing relationship with her, haven't you?"

"Long-standing, no. Bria and I knew each other when we were younger. It's part of the reason she felt comfortable hiring West Investigations when she realized she had a stalker. But before she contacted West Investigations two days ago, we hadn't spoken in fourteen years."

"But if you hadn't spoken to her in well over a decade, why would she seek you out?"

"That sounds like a question that should be directed at Ms. Baker," Brandon shot back.

This time it was Xavier who shot Brandon a hard glare. The last thing he wanted was for the detectives to get the idea that they should drag Bria down to the station and start questioning her.

"You've been staying at Ms. Baker's townhouse for the last few nights. Protecting her." Roslak smirked. "Is that correct?"

It took work to keep his expression neutral and not allow the detective to see his disdain. "That's correct."

"And Ms. Baker indicated in her statement that she told you the code to shut on and off her security system. Is that also correct?"

"It is."

Xavier watched a hint of concern flare in Brandon's eyes. "Get to the point, Detective."

"The point, counselor, is that I've been thinking

about this case long and hard." Roslak folded his hands behind his head and leaned back in his chair. "Ms. Baker thinks she has a stalker. She's filming in New York and seeks out an old flame. Someone she thinks might still have the hots for her. Someone who she could maybe manipulate with stories of old times and promises of new ones." Roslak let the insinuation hang in the air for a moment before plowing forward. "Mr. Steele traveled over three thousand miles to take pictures of Ms. Baker. That sounds pretty stalker-y to me. Maybe you, or Ms. Baker, thought he was your guy. Maybe you decided to take matters into your own hands. You use your firm's considerable resources to find the rental Mr. Steele is staying in and you eliminate Ms. Baker's stalker problem."

"Sounds like all you have is a whole bunch of speculation, Detective Roslak, and unless you have more than that, we're done here." Brandon stood.

Xavier followed his lead and stood as well.

"If you want to speak to my client again, call me first." Brandon nodded at each of the detectives, who remained seated. "Detectives." He gestured to Xavier to head for the interrogation room door.

They strode through the halls of the police station and out the front doors in silence.

Neither spoke until they were safely ensconced in Brandon's BMW and on the road back to West Investigations headquarters.

"So what do you think about all that back there?" Xavier finally asked.

Brandon shot a glance across the car. "They're grasping."

"That's good, right? Like you said, it means they don't really have anything."

"Maybe," Brandon said. "Our problem is that people who are grasping tend to be desperate, and desperate people will grab on to anything that looks like it could help them. And right now, it seems as if they're reaching for you."

Chapter Sixteen

Xavier had left with the police detectives more than three hours earlier and Bria spent most of that time pacing the conference room. Ryan had offered to have someone drive her home but she'd insisted on waiting for Xavier to return.

She'd wanted to call in the top New York criminal defense attorney, but Ryan had suggested she wait. His brother Brandon wasn't directly employed by West Security and Investigation, but he had plenty of experience dealing with the NYPD.

Waiting for Xavier to get back to West Investigations headquarters was like torture. They couldn't possibly think that Xavier had something to do with Bernie's death. She'd made it clear in her statement that Xavier had come to her room only moments after the sound outside had roused her from sleep. He couldn't possibly have gotten inside and upstairs that quickly. Not to mention she'd seen a car speeding away. Whoever killed Bernie had to have been in that car, and it wasn't Xavier.

She was on the verge of marching down to the police station and demanding they let Xavier go when he walked into the room.

She rushed toward him and into his arms without pausing to think. "Oh, thank goodness. I was starting to think they'd arrested you or something."

She felt some of the anxiety she'd been carrying since Xavier had left with the detectives seep out of her body as he wrapped his arms around her waist.

"Not quite," the man who'd walked into the room behind Xavier said.

Bria looked over Xavier's shoulder at the man with him. He looked enough like Ryan and Shawn West that she didn't need to guess that he was their older brother Brandon.

"Ryan said I had nothing to worry about since he was sending you to represent Xavier. I guess he was right."

Brandon West shot her a dazzling smile. All the West brothers were attractive enough to have solid careers in the entertainment industry, but she could immediately tell that Brandon West had that extra something, the "it" factor that was necessary to make star status. And he was a lawyer. There was probably some sort of irony in that, but she was too worried about Xavier at that moment to ponder it.

She turned to Xavier now. "Are you all right?"

"I'm fine." His arm was still around her waist. "It was just a few questions."

Bria studied Xavier's face. It had been fourteen years since they'd been truly close but she could still read him. It hadn't just been questions.

"This is where I take my leave of you," Brandon said, stretching a hand out to Xavier. "Call if you need me."

The two men shook and Brandon left them alone.

"What did they ask you?" Bria asked as soon as the conference room door closed.

"It was just some more routine questions about finding Bernie."

Bria pointed a finger at him. "No, don't do that. The cops don't show up at your job and take you to the station just to ask routine questions."

Xavier was silent for a moment, considering.

She crossed her arms and waited.

"They think I might have had something to do with Bernie's death."

"That's ridiculous!" The words exploded from her.

"Don't worry about it. It will be fine."

Bria began pacing again. "This is my fault. I dragged you into this, and now the police consider you a suspect in a murder."

"Hey." Xavier stepped in front of her, stopping her pacing. He took both her hands in his. "You are not at fault for any of this. The stalker or whoever killed Bernie is the only one at fault here. What we need to do is focus and find that person."

The feel of his hands in hers steadied her.

She nodded. "Okay."

Xavier let her hands fall to her side. "We're going to talk to Tate Harwood tomorrow morning. We still have a little time before you have to be at your interview with Ian Cole. What do you say we go try and speak with Robert Gindry now."

Bria agreed, and minutes later, they were on the road to Connecticut. They spoke very little, both of them lost in their own thoughts. So much had happened in such a short period of time, and no matter what Xavier said, she couldn't help feeling guilty about having pulled him into the mess that was currently her life.

Xavier pulled the car to a stop at the curb in front of a yellow brick colonial with black shutters. The lawn had been recently mowed, as evidenced by the neat vertical rows still visible in the grass, and the hedges on either side of the front door were trimmed to exactly the same height. The house was the picture of the quintessential American home.

"I'm stating, again, for the record, I don't like you being here," Xavier growled.

"And I'm stating, again, for the record, that I don't care. Now, are you ready?" Bria unlatched her seat belt and reached for the door handle.

"Wait. Let me come around first."

She rolled her eyes, but waited for Xavier to open the door for her. "Thank you."

Xavier closed the car door behind her and started

up the walkway. "If I say we're leaving, we're leaving, okay?"

"Fine, but I'm telling you, Rob is not my stalker. He was the nicest guy ever."

Xavier slanted her a look as she reached out to press the doorbell.

"People change," he said.

"You've never met Rob."

A moment later, the door opened and a girl of thirteen or fourteen stood in front of them. Her head was down, her gaze focused on the cell phone in her hand.

"Hi. I was hoping to speak to Rob Gindry. Is this his residence?" Bria asked.

"Yeah. May I ask who's—" The girl's head came up and she choked on the remainder of her sentence. She stared in shocked silence for a long moment before letting out an excited ear-piercing squeal. "Dad!"

Bria wasn't unaccustomed to this sort of greeting from some people when they realized who she was, but the girl's voice reached an octave that made her flinch all the same.

She felt Xavier tense next to her. She reached out and placed her hand on his arm. The teenager wasn't a threat to anything other than their eardrums.

A crash sounded from the second floor of the house and then footsteps thundered down the stairs. Rob came into view, a baseball bat clutched in his hand just as a brunette woman careened around the corner, a rolling pin in one hand and a cell phone in the other. Both parents were ready to fight to the death in defense of their offspring.

Xavier pulled her back several steps, positioning his body between Bria, Rob and the woman Bria assumed was Rob's wife.

He needn't have worried.

"It's Brianna Baker. Princess Kaleva, at our door." The girl jumped up and down, yanking on her mother's arm as she did. The woman looked confused, unsure of exactly what was going on. It didn't escape Bria's notice that she still held on to the rolling pin as if ready to smack someone in the head with it any second.

"Brianna Baker?" Rob let the baseball bat fall to his side, a wide grin blooming across his face. He turned to his family. "I told you I knew her!"

He leaned the bat against a wall, then stepped out of the house, sweeping Bria into a crushing hug. He pulled back after a long moment. "I can't believe you're standing on my porch. Come in. Come in."

Rob swept them into the house. "This is my wife, Alexandria." He motioned to the woman, who set the rolling pin on a side table and extended her hand.

"Nice to meet you," Alexandria said, her eyes still clouded with questions.

"And this is my daughter, Cleo, who I will be talking to about not screaming as if she's under attack unless she is actually under attack later today."

"OMG, Bria. I love you. Like, Princess Kaleva is such an empowering female character. All my friends love her. We've seen every one of the movies. I mean, I've seen all of your movies. Dad makes us watch them. He said he knew you from his acting days, but, like, I would have never imagined you'd show up at our house. I have to call Tiffany."

"No." Bria reached out and touched the teenager's hand, looking from her to her parents. "I am sorry to drop in on you like this, unannounced, but it would be better if no one knew I was here."

Cleo's face fell. "But my friends will never believe I met you if they don't see you for themselves."

Bria smiled at the girl. "How about I take as many selfies with you as you want, enough so that no one could ever doubt I was here, but you can't post them or show them to anyone until after I've left?"

Cleo considered it for a moment. "Deal."

Alexandria smiled and hooked an arm over her daughter's shoulder. "How about we go get refreshments for Brianna and…?"

"Oh, please excuse my poor manners. This is my friend, Xavier Nichols."

Rob, Xavier and Alexandria said their hellos. Cleo barely acknowledged his presence, her eyes were still full of stars and glued on Bria.

"Okay," Alexandria said, turning her daughter toward the back of the house. "Let's get those refreshments started."

Cleo reluctantly let her mother lead her away.

"Come, please, have a seat." Rob led them into a

sunny living room with two well-worn sofas facing each other.

Xavier followed them but didn't sit down. "Do you mind if I take a quick look around the house?"

Rob's brows went up to his receding hairline.

"Xavier is my friend, but he's also my bodyguard."

Rob's eyes swept over Xavier. "That makes sense." He shrugged. "Sure. Go ahead."

Xavier walked through the attached formal dining room and disappeared around a corner.

"Cleo isn't exaggerating, you know," Rob said sitting on the sofa across from Bria. "I do take the family to every one of your movies. I'm so happy you're doing so well."

"Thank you, Rob. And it looks like you're doing well too." Bria gestured, indicating the home around them.

Rob smiled, waving away the compliment. "I gave up on acting, which I'm sure you know. To be perfectly honest with you, I never had the talent to make a real go of it, and once I met Alexandria, I wanted to be able to build the life she deserved. We moved to Connecticut, where Alex is from, after we had Cleo. I sell insurance now."

"Well, your family and your home are beautiful. It looks like you made the right choice."

"I did. And look at you. You've definitely been making the right career choices. Princess Kaleva. Maybe I should have curtsied instead of hugging you."

Bria laughed. "No need for that."

"So, what brings you to see me? Don't get me wrong. I think you just earned me the father-of-the-century award, but I doubt you've sought me out just to raise my stature in my daughter's eyes."

Xavier returned to the living room. She waited until he sat to answer Rob's question.

"I don't know if you've seen the papers recently, but I'm having trouble with a stalker."

Rob leaned forward. "I hadn't seen that. I make sure to keep up with your movies, but I can't say that I read the gossip rags."

Bria smiled. "You're better off for avoiding them." Her smile fell away. "But this stalker, he's been sending me emails for a few months now and recently started sending flowers. With the last bouquet he sent a photo of me and Derek Longwell on the set of *Murder in Cabin Nine*."

Rob let out a slow breath. "Derek. I haven't thought about him in years. He was talented. His accident was such a shame."

"We're looking into whether the stalker's motivation might have something to do with the film or Derek Longwell's death," Xavier interjected. "We're hoping you can help us."

Rob leaned his elbows against his thighs. "I'll help in whatever way I can."

"Bria said you were close to Longwell back then. Was there anyone else who he was close to?"

"Derek wasn't the easiest person to be friends with," Rob said pointedly. "He had a huge ego. I mean, we were all struggling actors for the most part, but he came from money. Even though he wasn't a name, he'd never had to worry about how he was going to feed himself or make the rent. He was one of us, but the money also separated him from us, if you remember."

"I do," Bria said. "I remember we all stayed in that crappy motel close to the area where we filmed but Derek had a car so he stayed a couple towns over in a nicer hotel."

Rob pointed at her. "Exactly. He'd buy everyone's drinks for the night, but he wouldn't go back to the motel with us. One of us but not really one of us, you know."

"So how did you and Longwell become so close, then?" Xavier asked.

"I don't know if I'd say we became close. My wife says I've never met a person who wasn't a friend, and that's true to a point. I do find it easy to befriend people, but a lot of that is that I'm a good listener and I don't judge, at least not outwardly." Rob chuckled. "People like to tell me their problems. Derek was like that. Our friendship was based largely on his complaining to me about how horrible his stepfather and mother were."

"The stepfather who was bankrolling the movie he was in?"

Rob nodded. "Derek could be a lot of fun, but he was a spoiled brat. Constantly complaining about his parents, but he always took the money they gave him." Rob shrugged. "We were young."

Xavier cut a glance at Bria. They'd discussed how they were going to approach Derek's assault on her on the drive over. They needed to know if Rob could possibly be the stalker. If somehow he knew that Derek had planned to attack her or if he'd figured it out and this was his way of getting revenge for his friend. Bria hadn't bought into the possibility when Xavier floated it, and she was even surer that Rob had nothing to do with the stalking now. Still, she knew Xavier wouldn't be satisfied without asking Rob directly.

"Rob, I have to ask you something. It's about our time on the film." She'd agreed with Xavier that they wouldn't give specifics about Derek's assault. The last thing Xavier would want her to do was to give Rob the idea that she might have had something to do with Derek's death.

"Sure. Shoot," Rob said.

"Did you know that Derek tried to force himself on me?"

The stunned expression on Rob's face was more than enough to convince Bria that he'd had no idea.

Rob pushed to his feet. "No. Absolutely not. When?"

"I was able to fight him off and get away," Bria said, ignoring his question, "but it occurred to me recently that I might not have been the first woman he tried that with. Or the only woman he tried to assault on the set of the film. And as you said, people talked to you."

Rob paced a short line in front of his chair. "Bria, I promise you, if I'd known he'd attacked you, attacked anyone, I would have turned him in to the cops myself. Derek never said anything to me and neither did anyone else."

Bria believed him. They asked a few more questions but Rob didn't know anything that would help them.

She kept her promise and took several selfies with Rob's daughter and wife before saying goodbye to the family, apologizing for leaving without partaking of Alexandria's homemade scones, and promising to keep in touch with Rob.

"Rob was no help at all," she said, frustrated, when she and Xavier were back in the car.

"Hey, that's the nature of investigations. We just have to keep talking to people until we find someone who can help." Xavier reached across the console and pressed a kiss to her palm.

She tried to let his reasonableness soothe her, but as he pulled away from the curb, she couldn't help feeling things were going to get a lot worse.

Chapter Seventeen

A little over an hour after leaving Rob and his family, they were nearly at the Ritz. Xavier's phone rang. Ryan's name rolled across the in-dash screen. He accepted the call using the buttons on the SUV's steering wheel. "Bria and I just left Robert Gindry's place. I've got to get her to the hotel for her three o'clock interview, but I'd planned to call you while she did her thing and brief you on what we learned or, rather, didn't learn from him."

"I'm not calling about that." Ryan's voice came through the car's speakers. "The press has gotten wind that someone was killed at Bria's townhouse last night."

He glanced over at Bria. Her eyes were wide with shock.

He swore. "Bernie wasn't killed at Bria's house. He was killed somewhere else and his body was left in front of Bria's house."

"You wanna make that distinction for TMZ?"

Ryan shot back. "Bottom line is there's a horde of media in front of Bria's place right now."

Bria's phone rang. She snatched it from her purse and looked at the screen. "Mika. Probably calling to tell me exactly the same thing Ryan is saying right now." She declined the call.

Xavier swore again. "So the whole world knows where Bria lives now."

A breath whooshed out of Bria's lungs. He reached across the gearshift and took her hand, giving it what he hoped was a reassuring squeeze.

Bria's phone rang again. "Eliot. They are going to keep calling until I answer," she said before declining that call as well.

"It's not safe for her to go back to her place," Ryan said, stating the obvious.

"Copy that. We'll head into the office now. We can game plan our next steps when Bria and I get there."

"No." Bria shook her head. "I have to go to my interview."

Xavier glanced at her. "You can't still want to do that?"

"I didn't want to do the interview in the first place, but Eliot was right about the importance of controlling the narrative. It will be even more important now. And with the interview already set up, I can actually get a jump on framing the story."

A ball of frustration knotted in his chest. More Hollywood shenanigans.

Bria's phone rang again.

"It's Eliot. I'm going to take it and tell him the interview is still a go. If you can't drive me to the hotel, I'll call a car." Bria didn't make the statement as a threat but as a matter of fact.

He swore for a third time, but made the right turn at the next light that would take them to the Ritz-Carlton, where the interview was scheduled to take place.

"Thank you," she mouthed before punching the button on her phone to connect.

Xavier switched Ryan's call from the car's speakers to the Bluetooth headset in his ear. "You caught that?"

"Yeah." Ryan sighed. "You're on your way to the Ritz Carlton now?"

"Yes. We're about an hour away if traffic isn't too bad."

"Okay. I'm sending Gideon and Shawn to back you up. We know that the reporter who is meeting with Bria knows where she'll be. It seems unlikely that they'd have tipped off their colleagues to the location of the interview. They'd probably want to keep their exclusive to themselves, but I'm not taking any chances with Bria's safety."

"I agree. We checked out this reporter right?"

"Yeah. Bria's PR guy sent the name to us yesterday. He's clean."

"Be safe and keep your eyes open."

"Copy that." Xavier punched off the call with Ryan and a minute later Bria ended hers.

"Eliot has arranged for us to enter through the back of the hotel to avoid the other guests. He also spoke to the reporter interviewing me, who assured him that he hasn't shared the fact that he's doing the interview or the location with anyone other than his editor."

"Ryan's sending Shawn and Gideon to back me up. I'll tell them to meet us at the rear of the hotel."

He made the call.

They spent the rest of the ride in a flurry of text messages and phone calls. Mika and Eliot had already arrived and were waiting with a change of clothes for Bria in the suite where the interview would take place. The reporter hadn't arrived yet.

Shawn and Gideon were standing at the staff entrance of the hotel when Xavier pulled the SUV to a stop. Shawn opened the door for Bria while Gideon jogged around to the driver's side door as Xavier climbed from the car.

"I've got a secure spot to park. Then I'm going to scout the perimeter and set up a lookout point in the lobby," Gideon said.

"Good. We're in suite 1248. Stay on coms. I'm hoping this interview doesn't take too long." Xavier looked across the hood of the SUV. Shawn was leading Bria inside the hotel. His gut clenched as she disappeared behind staff entrance doors. He trusted Shawn, but he didn't want to let Bria out of his sight.

"Got it." Gideon climbed into the SUV and Xavier hustled toward the doors Shawn and Bria had disappeared through.

He caught up to them getting into the freight elevator. The elevator jerked them upward.

"Not exactly how I imagined an A-list movie star traveled," Shawn joked.

"You'd be surprised how many freight elevators I've been in," Bria shot back. "A lot of my glamorous lifestyle is nothing more than its own form of Hollywood magic."

"A bit of Hollywood magic a lot of people would love to experience."

Xavier was more concerned with reality than playing make-believe. "Did you check out the suite?" he said, focusing Shawn back on the task at hand.

"Yes. The suite and the eleventh, twelfth and thirteenth floors. No suspicious activity. Once we get Bria settled, I'll walk you through the paths of exit I've identified."

Xavier gave a terse nod. "Good."

"Guys, this is not a military mission. It's just an interview with an entertainment reporter. I've done a million of these things." She took his hand. "Everything will be fine. I'll be fine."

The elevator doors opened on the twelfth floor and Shawn took the lead, Xavier falling in behind

Bria so that she was sandwiched between the two of them. They made their way quickly to suite 1248.

Sykes and Mika rushed to Bria the moment she stepped inside.

"Don't you worry about a thing," Mika said, pulling Bria into the suite's living room. "Eliot and I are handling the vultures in front of your house as we speak."

Mika pulled Bria onto the sofa and she and Sykes fell down on either side of her.

"I've been on the phone for hours now, making sure that it's clear that you are the victim in this horrid situation," Sykes said.

Bria frowned. "I'm not sure that's accurate, given that Bernie is the one who was killed."

Something flashed over Sykes's face. Xavier didn't know him well enough to know whether it was anger or hurt, maybe both. But his features smoothed almost immediately. "Of course the dead man is the true victim of this crime. I just meant that I'm doing everything I can to make sure the press keeps the focus on that fact and acknowledges that you had absolutely nothing to do with this man's death."

Bria covered her agent's hand with her left hand and rested her right hand on Sykes's leg.

Xavier clenched his teeth against the jealousy that swelled in his chest.

"Thank you, both of you, for everything you've done for me. I know it's been a chaotic few days."

Sykes leaned over and pressed a kiss on Bria's cheek. "That's what we're here for. Anything you need, you just let me know."

"What I need right now is to get ready for this interview." Bria gave Sykes's leg a pat and rose.

Mika stood too, gesturing toward the closed doors of the suite's bedroom. "I got a couple of options from Alexander McQueen or, if you're feeling a bit riskier today, there's a Versace dress in the mix as well."

"I'm sure I'll find something that will work."

Bria disappeared into the bedroom to change.

Shawn ran Xavier through the exit scenarios he'd worked through in case they needed to get Bria out of the hotel quickly. Xavier would like to walk the planned escape routes himself, but there was no way he was leaving Bria's side.

The reporter showed as they were going through the plan.

Xavier left the greeting and setting up to Sykes and Mika, but that didn't stop him from studying the man who'd shown up.

Ian Cole was tall, blond and blue-eyed, and fit. He'd be no match for either he or Shawn if he did try something, but Ryan had said his background check had come up clean, so there was no reason to expect anything to go wrong.

Then, why was his gut churning?

Bria was right, she'd done tons of these interviews. The likelihood that the stalker would show up here was slim. Between Xavier, Shawn, Gideon, hotel security and all the many, many cameras throughout the hotel, attempting something here would be risky to the point of foolishness.

Which didn't mean the stalker wouldn't try. It might even make it more likely he would. Killing Bernard Steele had been risky and foolish and he'd done it anyway. It was clear the stalker was escalating and maybe even losing his grip on reality. Who knows what that might lead him to try.

The doors to the bedroom in the suite opened and Bria swept into the living room.

He had no idea whether she was wearing Alexander McQueen or whatever other designer outfit her agent had bought for her, but he knew she was breathtaking.

She'd chosen to wear a dark green jumpsuit with gold heels and matching gold jewelry. She'd pinned her long straight hair back and added large bouncy curls to the ends. She stepped out of the bedroom, her eyes sweeping over everyone in the room. Her gaze lingered on him for a moment before she crossed the room to greet the reporter.

His fingers ached with the need to touch her, but he hung back.

Just as Bria said, she was a pro at this. She handled the interview deftly, wrapping the reporter around her finger, exhibiting genuine grief over Bernie Steele's death and imploring whoever had a hand in it to come forward and turn themselves over to the police. The interview ended and Bria saw Ian Cole to the door. It was clear from the sappy look on Ian's face that the man was more than a little smitten with Bria.

Get in line, pal, he thought. Then, on second thought, *No, don't get in line. Bria is mine.*

He heard the words in his head, how they were almost exactly the same ones that the stalker had used in his note, and shuddered.

He wouldn't put himself in the same category as her stalker, no way. But thinking about Bria as his, that was objectifying her, thinking of her as something that could belong to him. Bria was and always had been her own person. She belonged to no one but herself and he wouldn't have it any other way.

As if she knew he was thinking about her, Bria looked over at him and winked.

No, she couldn't belong to anyone, but that didn't mean they couldn't be a team. Lifelong partners.

It was something he wanted to think about more but not now. Now his priority had to be Bria's safety. She couldn't go back to her townhouse. While she'd been doing the interview, he and Shawn had discussed the best place for her to stay.

They'd come up with an answer, but Xavier wasn't sure Bria would like it.

Bria closed the door behind the reporter and turned back to the room.

"You did amazing," Eliot said, crossing the room and pulling Bria into a hug that sent Xavier's jaw hardening.

"You did a wonderful job, darling," Mika said. "You had that reporter eating out of your hand. I'm sure the article will be very sympathetic toward you and everything you've been going through. Good news, since I hear that things haven't been going as smoothly as we might have liked on set." Mika's brows arched.

Bria frowned at her agent. "No movie ever runs smoothly. Things are just fine."

"Good." Mika gave Bria's shoulder a pat.

Someone knocked on the room's door.

Bria was closest to it, but Xavier stepped forward quickly, gently stopping her from reaching for the latch. He motioned for her to move back and looked out of the peephole.

A bellhop dressed in the uniform of the hotel stood in the hall. He held a long white box with a red bow.

Xavier opened the door.

"Hello, sir. A package arrived for Ms. Reynolds." The bellhop thrust the box at Xavier and waited expectantly.

After a moment, Sykes stepped up next to Xavier and thrust a wad of bills into the bellhop's hand before shutting the door.

Xavier turned to Mika. "This is for you."

Mika looked at him with an expression of surprise.

"Me? I can't imagine who'd be sending me something here."

Xavier sent a pointed look in Shawn's direction. "Do you mind if I open it?"

Mika waved a hand. "Go right ahead."

Xavier placed the box on the round table in the corner of the living room. Shawn came to stand to his right with Bria, Sykes and Mika standing on the other side of the table.

The fleeting thought that the package might be an incendiary device floated through his head, but that seemed unlikely, given the hands that the box had probably passed through on its way to the room.

Still, he lifted the top slowly, expending a small breath of relief when nothing exploded.

Relief quickly turned to anger as he processed what he was seeing inside the box.

Half a dozen black roses and a photo of him leading Bria into her townhouse. His face had been scratched out with a bloodred marker, and the word "die" scrawled across the bottom of the photo.

Chapter Eighteen

Bria leaned against the passenger door exhausted, thankful that no one could see her through the heavily tinted windows. Shawn, Xavier and Gideon had questioned the bellhop and every other hotel staff member who had handled the flowers, but no one knew anything helpful. Or at least, they weren't willing to share the information if they did. The only thing anyone could tell them was that the flowers had been delivered by a man in dark clothing and a ball cap pulled low over his forehead and eyes. The hotel security feed had confirmed that, but the man had been careful to keep his head down. The camera hadn't captured an image of him that was clear enough to be recognized. He carried a clipboard and looked like every other delivery person in New York City, according to the concierge who'd signed for the box. They'd gleaned one ominous clue from the concierge, however. The man had expressly stated that the package was for Ms. Reynolds in suite 1248, which meant he knew that Mika had reserved the room.

She hadn't wanted to believe someone close to her could be her stalker when Xavier suggested it, but now? Mika had insisted that, aside from Ian Cole, only she, her assistant and Eliot knew which hotel and room the interview would be taking place in. Xavier was having Ryan confirm with Ian that he hadn't let the meeting place and time slip to someone, but she knew he hadn't. In her experience, reporters were compulsive about protecting information regarding an exclusive interview. No way would a reporter have risked the competition finding out about the meeting and crashing it.

Which made it all the more likely that somehow, someone she trusted was betraying her in a terrifyingly upsetting way.

Bria opened her eyes and glanced across the car at Xavier. Not for the first time since this whole ordeal began, she was thankful that she'd gone to him for help. Even after their breakup and the years that had passed, he was the one person in the world she knew she could count on, no matter what. And at the moment, he was the only person she trusted completely.

And that made her wonder about the choices she'd made in her life up until now. Sure, she had fame and fortune. She'd achieved her goal of becoming an actress, and not just one who could pay the bills but one who'd never have to worry about paying the bills again. An actress with influence in the industry. A role model for other little Black girls to look up to and know they could achieve their dreams too if they were willing to work hard for it.

But she was also isolated. Surrounded by studio executives, agents, PR people and fans but very much alone when she bore down to the root of it all. When she'd needed help the most, she'd had to reach back fifteen years to get it. What did that say about the life she'd chosen for herself?

She knew what it said about the man she'd left behind for that life. It said that he was caring and generous beyond what she likely deserved.

It said that she'd made a mistake leaving him all those years ago.

She shook the thought from her head. She wouldn't have the career she had if she had stayed.

But what about now?

She had the career. The influence. The money. Maybe now she could have the man too.

"What?" Xavier said, breaking into her reverie.

"What, what?"

"Why are you looking at me like that? If you're worried, don't be. I'm not going to let anything happen to you."

"I know that." She sighed. "Do you think that the police will be able to find the delivery guy?"

At Ryan West's insistence, Xavier had called the police and they'd filed a report after he and Shawn had questioned the hotel staff. With Bernie being killed and left in front of her house not long after the confrontation with Xavier, Ryan felt that it was in Xavier's best interest to have everything on the record. There were too many innocent men in prison for Bria to be sure he was right about that, but Xavier had agreed with his boss.

"No. I don't think they'll look too hard either. No crime was committed. But filing a report puts on the record that you are being stalked."

"Yippee."

Xavier made a left turn and took the ramp for the Holland Tunnel.

"Where are we going?"

He shot a glance at her before focusing back on the road in front of him. "Your place isn't safe. Too many people know about it now, and the press are probably still lurking if they aren't just camping out there."

"I agree." As much as she hated it, her beloved townhouse just wasn't safe for her at the moment. "But you didn't answer my question."

"I'm taking you to my place."

Her stomach did a flip-flop. She wanted to see Xavier's place. To see how he lived. But spending the night at his place felt…emotionally dangerous. On some level, she knew it wasn't all that different from him staying at hers, but at her townhouse, she was on her own home turf.

"I don't have a change of clothes."

"I can have a female operative at West Investigations pick up some things for you."

"That would be great. Thank you." She smiled, relieved that one thing was easily handled, since there was so much else in her life at the moment that couldn't be.

"I'll make the call now. While I'm at it I'll also order us something for dinner. Anything in my fridge is well past its best-by date. Is Chinese food good for you?"

"Perfect."

He made the calls.

"Are you sure it's safe? I mean, people have seen you and I together. The stalker or the press might think I'd be hiding out at your place and look up your address."

Xavier arched an eyebrow. "They could look, but they won't find it. I own it through a private company."

"Ah." She smiled. "I totally get that." She'd had to purchase her townhouse in a similarly circumspect manner.

"Trust me. I have a top-of-the-line security system, my neighbors mind their own business and I have a friend across the street who is former Special Forces. It's unlikely anyone would find you here, but if they somehow do, they're in for a surprise. You can relax."

Relax. She was starting to forget what that felt like. But if she was going to relax with anyone, it would be with Xavier.

Her body heated at the thought of just how relaxed he used to make her.

Forty-five minutes later, Xavier pulled into the driveway of a small bungalow in a New Jersey suburb and hit a button on his sun visor that sent the garage door opening. He pulled the car in, shut off the engine and closed the door before getting out and leading her into a mud room off the kitchen.

The open space living room/dining room/kitchen felt more like a loft than a single family home. The peaked ceiling was lined with dark wood beams and a stone fireplace climbed the far wall. A brown leather sectional sofa was positioned so it faced a flat screen television but also took advantage of a large bay window looking out on the backyard. A wood-topped table that matched the beams overhead anchored the dining space, and the kitchen looked as if it had been newly remodeled with light granite countertops and stainless steel appliances.

"Your home is gorgeous."

"Thanks," Xavier said, flipping on the lights in the living room. "It didn't look so gorgeous when I bought it five years ago. I did a lot of work to whip it into shape."

"Well, it definitely paid off. It's very warm and comfortable."

"I'm glad you think so." He smiled. "And you should. You know, make yourself comfortable. Here, let me show you to the guest room."

He pointed out his bedroom as he led her down a short hall off the main room. Xavier kept walking but she paused at his door. Just as with the main living area, his room was masculine but lived-in. A king-size mahogany bed sat against the longest wall in the room flanked by matching, round bedside tables. A five-drawer dresser completed the set. From the doorway she could see into the small en suite bathroom, which also looked as if it had been recently updated with white marble flooring and a glass-enclosed shower.

Her mind jumped to an image of falling into the bed with Xavier, the soft linens at her back, his lust-covered face looming over her. Desire ran through her core.

"You're welcome to sleep here if you prefer it to the guest room."

She jumped at the sound of Xavier's husky baritone in her ear.

Heat flooded her face. There was no hiding what she'd been thinking. "I was just taking a look."

"Look all you want."

She moved toward him, going onto her toes and pressing her lips against his, softly at first, but when he responded, she deepened the kiss. His hands roamed down her sides, to her hips to cup her butt. She didn't want him to stop. She was edging them into the bedroom when the doorbell rang.

Xavier managed to pull back.

"That's dinner."

Another delivery person with terrible timing. She

sighed internally. This was one time she wouldn't have minded having dessert before dinner.

She waited until Xavier had paid for the food and shut the door firmly before stepping out of the hallway. He didn't need to tell her that it was important that as few people as possible knew where she was staying.

He grabbed plates, silverware and cups while she took the food from the bags and peeked into the cartons to see what he'd gotten. She hadn't paid much attention while he was ordering the food, but she wasn't surprised to see that he remembered her favorite dishes. Peking duck. Scallion pancakes. Dumplings. It was all here. More food than they could probably eat in two nights.

The smell hit her, reminding her it had been several hours since her last meal. Her stomach growled in anticipation and they both spent the next several minutes eating in comfortable silence.

"Thank you for letting me stay in your home," Bria said once she'd had enough food to take the edge off her hunger. She reached for the bottle of red wine Xavier had opened and poured herself a half glass.

"You're welcome. You're always welcome here."

She studied his face but found nothing there except honesty. "You really mean that, don't you?"

"Of course I do."

"Even after how things ended between us?"

He let out a long breath. "That was a long time

ago. I admit, seeing you again brought some of those old feelings, that old resentment up again. But you did what was best for you at the time, and obviously, it paid off."

She traced the ridge of her wineglass with her index finger. "I don't regret choosing my career then. At the time, I couldn't have managed acting and having a relationship. It was never about you though. It was always about what I had the capacity to handle at one time back then."

And now she wanted both. The thought raced through her head. She wanted him and her career. But she knew it might be too late for that.

"I get it. In a very real way, your decision was the best thing for both of us. I wouldn't have gone into the military if you hadn't dumped me."

"Really? I've been meaning to ask you how you ended up enlisting. I don't remember you mentioning wanting to join the army."

As much as her breaking up with him had hurt, the one silver lining was that it had led to his enlisting in the army. He'd never be sorry about that. "Because I hadn't even considered it until the night you broke up with me."

Her mouth formed a shocked O.

"I somehow found myself in Bryant Park that night, after you gave me my walking papers. I don't even remember getting off the subway, but I was sitting in the park, well after midnight, when a police officer found me."

"The park closes at night."

"That's exactly what he said. But he also saw that something was wrong. To this day, I don't know why but I just unloaded everything on him. My dead-end job. My girl breaking up with me. Everything. And Officer Jarell Hurt, who'd only gotten out of the army a few years prior, suggested that if I was looking for something to take my mind off a broken heart and a new career path that the army could be for me. Turned out it was one of the best decisions I've ever made."

"Wow, that's some story."

"Jarell is a good man. He's retired now, but we still get together regularly for a beer or to watch the game on television."

"Does he know Brianna Baker is the girl who broke your heart?"

Xavier looked away. "I told him." He picked up his empty plate and carried it to the kitchen sink.

She grabbed her plate and followed him. She reached across him and set her plate on top of his in the sink. Turning so there were only inches between them, she looked up at him. "And now? Are you going to tell him I'm back in your life?"

His hands fell onto her shoulders. "Are you back in my life?"

Chapter Nineteen

Bria stood pressed against him, her heart pounding against his chest. The need to sweep her off the ground and carry her to his bedroom was nearly overwhelming. He'd had sexual partners other than her, but he'd only ever experienced a need so palpably strong with her. From the look in her eyes, she felt it too.

Somewhere in the back of his mind, he realized becoming intimate with Bria again could be a bad idea. It would most likely lead to him alone with a broken heart just as it had before. But drowning in her beautiful brown eyes, heartbreak seemed a small price to pay to have her in his bed once more. Then she drew even closer, pressing her pelvis against his already stiff length and all reason flew out the window.

"I want you, Xavier." The way she said his name made him long to hear her say it again, but this time, as he thrust himself inside of her. "Tell me you want me too."

It wasn't a profession of love, but it was enough for him right now. More than enough.

He held her tightly against him. "You can feel how much I want you." He rested his forehead against hers. "But there's no going back if we do this."

"There's been no going back from the moment I saw you again. At least not for me."

That was all he needed to hear. "It's always been you, Bri. Always." He dipped his head down and claimed her mouth. She tasted like heaven.

Her hands traveled down his chest and across his hips until she gripped his backside. He grabbed the hem of her sweater and pulled it over her head, letting it fall to the kitchen floor. She wore a sheer, lacy black bra and when he dipped his hand under the material and cupped her breast, massaging her nipple with his thumb, she let her head fall back and moaned.

It was the most erotic and beautiful thing he'd ever seen.

"You are so damn gorgeous. Do you know that?"

She looked at him. "I missed this. I missed you."

Something inside of him melted at her words.

He swept her into his arms, taking her mouth in a hot, heavy kiss and carried her to his bedroom. He set her down in front of his bed. "I missed you too, sweetheart. So much more than I can say. But I plan to show you just how much."

He found her mouth again while her hands worked at the button of his jeans. Moments later, their clothes were littered across his bedroom floor and he finally had her where he wanted her. In his bed.

He took his time, his hands exploring. He brought his mouth to one breast and then the other, lavishing her nipples with the adoration they deserved. She was all curves and softness, a contrast to his hard edges, but somehow, they fit. At that moment, he would give anything to know that she would be in his bed every night for the rest of his life. But if all they had was tonight, he was determined to make it memorable.

He kissed his way down her body and then back up again until he worked his way to the sensitive flesh on the inside of her thigh. He felt her shudder in anticipation and his already painfully tight groin pulsed with need.

"Xavier, please. I need you now." Her face was flushed with desire.

He was determined that she should have her pleasure before he took his, so he focused on her luscious body.

He slid his hands beneath her bottom and tilted her up, bringing his mouth to her core. She was more than ready for him and it didn't take long for her to find her release. Her muscles clenched and her body vibrated as she tipped over the edge, screaming his name.

BRIA WAS STILL coming down from the climax Xavier had sent shooting through her body when he reached over to the nightstand and took out a condom. Watching him sheath himself renewed the never-ending desire she seemed to have for him. She hadn't been exaggerating when she'd told him she'd wanted him from the moment she'd seen him again. If she was being totally honest, she'd never stopped wanting him.

Now here he was, crawling up her body, seating himself at her opening. And she craved nothing more than to feel him inside of her, tipping her over the edge with desire again, and again, and again.

She reached out for him, guiding him to where she wanted him, opening her legs to accommodate his size. Her gaze was locked on his face, not wanting to miss his expression the moment he entered her for the first time in far too long.

He gave a guttural moan as he thrust himself inside of her. She opened wider, taking him in fully, adjusting for his girth and length. He felt amazing. So much better than she could have ever imagined.

And then he began to move inside of her, and all thought fled. All she could do was feel. And it felt so damned good.

Far too soon, she felt her body tensing again.

Xavier smiled down at her as a second orgasm rocketed through her body. And then his smile faded as he thrust into her harder, faster, deeper, barreling toward his own release.

She thrust her hips in time with him, wanting to give him as much pleasure as he'd given her, riding a third wave building inside of her.

Their bodies exploded in time with each other. She felt him pulsing inside of her even as the walls of her core clenched around him.

Xavier rolled onto his side, breathing hard and pulling her in close to him. Her heart raced along with his and she pressed a kiss to his chest. She lay in his arms, wanting to share with him what she was feeling at that moment. Wanting to say those three little words she should have said fifteen years ago.

But she didn't. Because those three little words weren't all that mattered.

They'd both built lives for themselves far away from each other, and at some point, they'd have to return to those lives. But maybe they could figure out a way. Other people did it. Why couldn't they?

But she didn't have to think about that now.

She wrapped her arms around Xavier and held him tightly. For now she could pretend that this, the two of them right here, would never end.

Chapter Twenty

Bria was still asleep in his arms when Xavier woke. Part of him wished he could stay where he was, holding her. He knew waking up next to her was temporary, but he couldn't help wishing that it wasn't.

Instead of dreaming dreams that couldn't be, he got out of the bed, taking care not to wake Bria, and headed for the bathroom. Showered and dressed, he reentered the bedroom, only to find the bed empty.

He found Bria in the kitchen, sipping freshly brewed coffee from one of his favorite mugs. She was barefoot and wearing the shirt he'd shed in a hurry before taking her to bed the evening before.

"I hope you don't mind," she said, a hint of hesitation in her tone. "I made coffee."

He crossed the kitchen and bent to place a kiss on her lips. "I don't mind at all."

He poured a mug for himself. "Tess, one of my coworkers, is going to bring you some clothes to wear. She should be here soon. Hopefully, the press mob has moved on and we can get back into your place sometime today."

"To stay? Or just for me to pick up a few things?"

"I think it's best if you stay here for the time being. Even if the press has backed off, your address is out in the public now. I want West to do a full security sweep and assessment. Your security was good, but you'll probably have to level up now."

Bria rubbed her temple with the hand that wasn't holding her mug. "Whatever you need to do."

He shot off a quick text to Ryan asking him to take care of the sweep.

Bria sat her mug on the counter. "I missed a call from Tate Harwood last night."

The slight smile on her lips told him she was thinking about what they'd been doing when the call must have come in. The memory put a matching grin on his face.

"Is that so?"

She swatted at him and he dodged out of the way.

"Tate says he's available to see us anytime today."

He couldn't keep the surprise off his face. "Really? It was that easy."

Bria's smile grew wider. "I told you he'd be falling all over himself to take the meeting. It probably helped that I hinted at maybe having a project I was interested in talking to him about."

"Okay, and how is he going to react when he finds out there is no project?"

Bria shrugged. "He won't be happy, but he'll get over it."

The doorbell rang.

"That's Tess."

Bria headed for the hallway leading to the bedrooms. "I'll call Tate back and set up a meeting for this morning. I have to be on set by two today." She disappeared down the hall.

He went to the front door, and after checking that it was in fact Tess standing on his porch, he let her in.

Tess's gaze moved around his home in a practiced, efficient scan. "Nice. We should have a company happy hour or two here."

He arched an eyebrow. "I don't think so."

Tess laughed and handed him the shopping bags she held in her hands. "Not a lot open this early in the morning. Had to hit the big box store. Nowhere near as nice as the stuff that Bria is used to wearing, but it'll do until she can get her own things."

"Thanks. I know she appreciates it."

Tess cocked her head to one side. "Huh. So."

He didn't like the way she was looking at him. "Huh. So. What?"

"The two of you are hitting the sheets. Honestly, I saw it coming a mile away, but Ryan won't be happy."

Xavier turned his back to her. He'd never been the kind of man to kiss and tell and he wasn't going to start now. "You don't know what you're talking about."

Tess laughed. "Okay, but I'll give you some advice. If you want to have a chance that Ryan doesn't pick up on the fact that you're doing the midnight rumba with a client, you should tap into your growly side some more. You are far too chill, for you, to convince anyone you haven't recently gotten laid."

He turned back to Tess with a scowl on his face.

"There he is. That's what I'm talking about." She laughed again.

"Thanks for the clothes. Now, get out."

Tess left, still laughing.

He carried the bags into the bedroom, catching Bria still on the phone with Harwood.

Even though she didn't have the call on speakerphone, Xavier could clearly hear Harwood's excitement on the other side of the line. He agreed to meet with Bria in his office in an hour.

"The power of being an A-list celebrity," Bria said after ending the call.

"An A-list ego to match," he teased.

"Gotta have something to balance out the self-doubt."

"Just make sure you use the power for good and not evil."

"Always," Bria shot back with a sexy smile that made his insides melt.

He left her to shower and change while he again read through the background information they'd compiled on Harwood.

Bria reappeared in the living room forty-five minutes later in skinny jeans, a fancy off the shoulder shirt and black pumps. Her hair was up in a complicated twist and her makeup looked expertly applied. It was simple, classic, but she still looked like a million bucks.

"Wow, you look great."

She beamed. "Tate's online bio with Panthergate Productions lists him as a producer. But based on my experience, that could mean anything from he's a glorified coffee boy to he's the brains of the operations. In either case, he'll undoubtedly want to exploit our renewed relationship to up his clout within the company."

"Tough business," Xavier said, taking the oversize sweater she carried in her arms from her and holding it open so she could shrug into it.

He wrapped the material around her shoulders and she turned slightly, leaning back against him and looking up at him with a wink. "Thanks."

He pressed a kiss to her neck and she sank back farther.

"What do you say to going back to bed?"

He pressed a kiss to the other side of her neck.

"I don't think we have time for what you're thinking," Bria said teasingly.

"You know you're thinking about it too," he teased.

She giggled. "Maybe, but we still don't have time now. Later."

He sighed and stepped back, letting his hands fall from her shoulders.

Bria turned and faced him. "When we get to Tate's office, let me do the talking, okay? He's bound to be a little put out when he realizes the project I mentioned to him on the phone is looking into Derek's murder, but he won't want to jeopardize our renewed acquaintance."

Xavier quirked an eyebrow. "So I'm to act like nothing more than your obviously lethal, devastatingly handsome bodyguard?"

She grinned. "Whose ego is showing now?"

He grinned. "Is madam ready to go?"

Bria grabbed her handbag and slid it onto her wrist. "She is."

The Panthergate Productions offices were on the east side of Manhattan, but they weren't far. Traffic was merciful and they arrived only fifteen minutes late. The building offered valet parking, and Xavier slipped the valet a fifty to keep the car in front of the building although he was pretty sure the young man would have done it for nothing more than the smile Bria shot him as she'd gotten out of the SUV.

Xavier strode into the building at Bria's side. It was as if she was a magnet, compelling all of the heads in the lobby to turn toward her. An excited buzz hummed through the air.

He swept his gaze over the mostly suit-clad people, most likely employees of the production company coming or going to lunch or meetings. None of the faces held a threat. They mostly reflected excitement.

A heavyset, middle-aged man in a light brown suit hurried through the security gate toward them. Xavier recognized him as Tate Harwood. The face was the same as the photo he'd seen in the background check Ryan had pulled, even if the man was now thirty pounds heavier and ten years older. His hair was almost completely gray with only a few stray patches of dark brown pushing through. The crow's feet around his eyes were the bigger indicator of his age, which Xavier knew was fifty-two.

"Brianna Baker," Harwood boomed in a voice just a touch louder than it needed to be. "How are you? How long has it been? Too long, much too long."

It wasn't at all subtle, but a glance at the faces watching them revealed that it was working. The gazes of the people in the lobby moved between Brianna and Harwood, alight with curiosity about the man who somehow knew Brianna Baker personally.

"Tate." Brianna air-kissed Harwood on either cheek without actually touching him. "You are so right. It has been too long. When I learned you were back in New York and working at a production company, I just knew I had to reach out to you."

Harwood folded her arm around his and began to lead her toward the bank of elevators. "And I am so glad you did." He sent a glance over his shoulder, taking in Xavier, who had fallen into step behind them.

"Oh, I hope you don't mind. Xavier goes everywhere with me. Personal security. You know how it is." Bria tapped Harwood's arm lightly. "Such a pain, but I trust him implicitly."

"Of course," Harwood said, sparing Xavier one more look before focusing all his attention on Bria. "And this is my assistant, Mary Beth." Harwood gestured to the woman who was holding the elevator doors open and waving off anyone who tried to enter.

They stepped onto the elevator and the doors slid closed before the elevator car started its smooth climb upwards.

"I've had Mary Beth order in refreshments from Pâtisserie la Reine. I remembered how much you like dessert," Harwood said.

"Oh, that is so sweet of you. Of course, I have to watch what I eat so closely now, I'm not allowed to eat half of what I really want to." Bria laughed the tinkling laugh he recognized from her interviews.

"The price of fame." Harwood joined in laughing with her.

The elevator stopped at the twenty-third floor, and Harwood led them into a glass-walled conference room. He clearly wasn't going to let a drop of reflected importance go unnoticed.

Bria seemed to be taking it all in stride. She may have been used to living in a fishbowl, but Xavier wasn't. Even though Harwood had firmly closed the door after they'd entered the conference room, Xavier remained uncomfortable with the number of people strolling down the hall and gawking from the other side of the glass.

Harwood's assistant bought in coffee and the pastries. Bria accepted the coffee and demurred on the pastry.

No one offered him refreshments at all. He did as Bria asked and took up a position in a corner of the room, faced the glass wall and faded into the background.

After several minutes of small talk and catching up, Bria got down to why they were there.

"Tate, I'm sure you're wondering why I called you out of the blue today."

"Well, I am a little curious, yes."

"The truth is the project I'm working on involves *Murder in Cabin Nine* and Derek Longwell's untimely death."

Harwood flinched.

"I know it's a tragedy that those of us who knew Derek were all affected so deeply by. Especially those of us working on *Murder in Cabin Nine* with him. I mean, you know how the cast and crew on a film can become family. We were the people closest to him in his last days and moments."

"Yes, well, the industry lost a great up-and-coming talent in Derek," Harwood said unconvincingly.

Bria leaned forward across the table. "I've been thinking about starting a production company. You know how brutal this business is, especially to women, and a Black woman, well, I've got—what? Maybe five to seven more years left as a lead actress."

Harwood nodded. "Your talent and skill as a performer is timeless and boundless. But I can't argue with the fact that this business favors youth over talent."

"Exactly." Bria slapped a hand against the lacquered tabletop. "I want to plant my feet firmly in the industry soil. Producing my own content would do that."

Harwood cocked his head, a look of confusion coming over his face. "Are you thinking about reviving *Murder in Cabin Nine*?"

"Heavens no. The script was terrible. I'm thinking about telling Derek's story. The up-and-coming actor whose career and life were ended in a haze of mystery far too early. Audiences love what-could-have-been stories. I mean, we are still seeing massive audiences for biopics about Marilyn Monroe decades after her death."

"Derek was no Marilyn Monroe."

"No, of course, he never had a chance to achieve what she did, but ten years ago, he was probably the equivalent of Tom Holland or Harry Styles. He could have been, at least, and that's all that's needed to make a compelling story. What could have been?"

"Maybe." Harwood's eyes darted around the room. He smoothed his tie. "I'm not sure what I can do to help you," he said, his tone decidedly chillier than it had been moments earlier.

"As much potential as Derek had, I think you and I both know that he wasn't perfect, and if I want to do this biopic right, I have to tell a balanced story. The good and the bad."

"I…I still don't see where you're going…"

Bria sucked in a deep breath and then let it out slowly. "I never told anyone this at the time, but Derek attempted to force himself on me. I was able to fight off his attack."

Harwood's back straightened. "I didn't know anything about it. I hope you know that if I had I would have fired him immediately. Father producer or no father producer."

Bria waved a hand. "As I said, I never told anyone. Times were very different then. But that's why I'm sure that I wasn't the only woman Derek pulled that crap with. You worked with Derek several times on several different films. I figured you might know of other women who had similar experiences."

Harwood pulled at his tie again and didn't look Bria in the eye. "I did work with Derek on a number of films, but I wouldn't have tolerated such behavior if I'd known…"

"Of course, you would have." Bria cut him off sharply. "Derek was your bread and butter. But I have no plans to use the biopic to focus on what you did or didn't do years ago. At least, not at the moment."

Xavier smirked internally at Bria's interrogation technique.

Harwood swallowed hard, his Adam's apple bobbing. "What do you want to know?"

"Was there anyone you can remember who might have known that Derek attacked me? Anyone he was close to on set?"

Harwood scoffed. "You were there. Derek wasn't close to anyone. He didn't have friends. Thought he was too good for everyone."

"He could be full of himself," Bria agreed.

"That's a kind way of putting it. He was a class-A jerk." Harwood sighed. "Look, I'll admit I'd heard rumors about Derek's heavy-handedness with women, but I knew nothing about him attacking you. And as far as friends who might have known, I can't help you. Hell, Derek's own stepfather didn't like him. Talked about him like he was something he'd scraped off his shoe. That's probably where Derek learned it from. Do you remember how he treated that one guy who worked on the film with us?"

Xavier's ears perked up.

Bria's brow furrowed. "What guy?"

"Oh, you must remember him. He had a small part, only a couple of lines. What was his name? Now, him I did have to talk to Derek about, get him to back off a little at least. Nice guy but very awkward, kind of quiet. The kind of guy bullies love because he's not going to fight back."

Everyone eventually fought back, that was one thing that Xavier learned. Some people just had a greater tolerance, but they also tended to be the people most likely to explode when they finally reached their limit.

"What was his name?" Harwood looked at the ceiling, thinking. After a moment, he snapped his fingers and grinned. "Morgan Ryder. I'm surprised you don't remember him, Brianna. Now that you've stirred up all these memories from the movie set, the one thing I remember about Morgan in addition to how badly Derek treated him is how big a crush Morgan had on you."

Bria shot a glance across the room at Xavier. "I don't remember him."

Harwood shrugged. "He was that kind of guy. Forgettable, I mean. It's funny though. I ran into him a few years back when I was still living in Los Angeles. He'd completely changed. Slick suit. Two-hundred-dollar haircut. Nice ride. A real poor-guy-makes-it-big transformation."

"I guess that's good for him," Bria said.

"Sure. It's great. Like I said, nice guy. Totally deserves it. I almost didn't recognize him and he seemed surprised when I did. He'd even changed his name or I guess stopped using his stage name. Morgan Ryder." Harwood guffawed. "He's still in the business, kind of. Owns his own PR firm. Eliot Sykes Public Relations."

Chapter Twenty-One

Xavier threw the door to Ryan's office open, pausing long enough to allow Bria to enter first before he strode inside with purpose. "Eliot Sykes is the stalker."

"We don't know that for sure." Ryan sat behind his desk, working on his computer.

Shawn was also in the office, tapping away on a laptop on the sofa.

"I'm sure," Xavier growled.

He'd called Ryan on the drive from Tate Harwood's office and briefed him on his and Bria's meeting with Harwood. Ryan had apparently briefed Shawn.

"I'm working on tracking down this Morgan Ryder. So far, no luck. I've got Tansy working on it also. She's better at scouring the bowels of the internet."

Tansy Carlson was the best computer tech and researcher that West Investigations had. If anyone could dig up proof that Eliot Sykes and Morgan Ryder were one and the same person, it was Tansy.

"I've tried calling Eliot," Bria said. "He's not picking up his cell phone."

"And his office says he hasn't been in contact for the last two days."

Shawn's head snapped up. "Two days. That means he's been off the grid since the paparazzo was dumped outside of Bria's house."

"Oh my…" Bria pressed her hand against her stomach as if keeping the contents from coming up. "I hadn't even thought about what it means if Eliot really is my stalker. He must have killed Bernie." She sat down hard in one of Ryan's visitors' chairs.

Ryan looked across his desk at her with sympathy in his eyes. "We will find him. And until then, we will keep you safe from him."

Xavier felt every one of Ryan's words right down to his bones.

Tansy burst into the office. "I've got it." She had a wide grin across her face and held a printout above her head triumphantly.

"You found Sykes?" Xavier advanced on her.

Tansy took a step back, confusion coloring her face. "What? No, sorry. I meant I found the proof that Sykes and Ryder are the same person." She held out the printout.

Xavier took it. It was a copy of a very old web page that appeared to have been focused on discussing Hollywood celebrities. The sheet of paper was full of comments about Morgan Ryder. A small, grainy, indecipherable thumbnail photo was in the top left corner, but when he flipped to the second page he found Tansy had managed to blow the picture up and print it out. It was still grainy, but it was without a doubt Eliot Sykes, aka Morgan Ryder.

"I bookmarked the site so we could get back to it whenever we needed to," Tansy said.

Xavier passed the sheets of paper to Ryan. "This has to be enough to take to the cops."

Ryan scanned the papers. "It proves Sykes is Ryder, but it doesn't prove that Sykes is the stalker. We need more before the police will do anything."

Xavier hissed out a breath. He knew Ryan was right.

"He lied to me," Bria said. "If nothing else, by omission. He must have known we'd worked together on *Murder in Cabin Nine* and he said nothing for nearly two years. That's something."

"Fire him. In fact, I strongly suggest you do, but it's not illegal to lie to your employer."

"I'd hold off on firing him." Shawn rose and joined them at Ryan's desk. "We don't know if he knows we suspect him. We may be able to use that."

"He's not answering Bria's calls," Xavier pointed out.

Shawn's mouth twisted into a grimace. "I said 'may be able to use that.' It looks like Bernie's murder has pushed Sykes past the point of playing the good guy PR rep. He may be fully engulfed in his own decisions about being with Bria and has completely jettisoned his outward life."

"Oh…" Bria pressed a hand over her mouth.

Ryan shot Shawn a hard look.

"Sorry," Shawn mouthed back.

"I think I need to freshen up." Bria rose.

"I'll show you where the ladies' room is." Shawn hurried to extend his arm to Bria and she took it with a small smile of thanks.

When they were gone, Xavier turned back to Ryan. "We have to do something now."

Ryan stood, came around his desk and faced Xavier. "We are doing something. We're protecting Bria. We're searching for Eliot. We're staying diligent. That's all we can do at the moment."

"It's not enough," Xavier growled.

"I didn't say it was. It's what we have." Ryan hesitated. "Remember when I said that you were too close to Bria to be responsible for her security?"

Xavier didn't respond. There was no way he was going to desert Bria now.

"I know you're not going to leave her protection to anyone else," Ryan said, reading his mind. "I'm just reminding you that if you let your emotions do the thinking, you aren't going to be as effective as Bria needs you to be."

"I can separate my emotions from my job."

Ryan scoffed. "Right. Like you've been doing? Everyone can see what you feel for Bria. And I can tell it's affecting you."

He wanted to deny it, but he couldn't. He wasn't

thinking as clearly as he would be if he was protecting anyone other than Bria. All he could think about was what he'd do if she got hurt or worse. He'd survived fifteen years without her, in part because he believed they were both doing what they were supposed to be doing with their lives. If they couldn't do it together, well, at least they were happy-ish apart.

But the thought of a world without Bria in it… He was sure he couldn't make it through an hour in that world. So he'd give his life to make sure that was a world that never existed.

"I can't deny I have feelings for Bria. Always have, always will. But we had our chance and she chose her career over me. We can't change that and I doubt she wants to. She'll go back to Hollywood when this is all over and I'll still be here. So whatever is going on between us now, it can't last."

Ryan's gaze moved to the office door.

Xavier turned even though he already knew what he'd find.

Bria stood there, Shawn behind her. Her back was ramrod straight, hurt shining in her eyes. She'd clearly heard every word he'd just said.

Damn. He hadn't meant to hurt her, but he'd only said out loud what they both knew to be true. Hadn't he?

The moment of silence seemed to go on forever before Bria spoke. "There's been a change in the shooting schedule. They need me on the set."

Shawn cleared his throat, nodding at Xavier. "If you want to stay here and keep searching for Sykes, I can take her."

"No. I'll do it," Xavier said.

"Thank you." Bria's response was icy enough to skate on. She turned, sending Shawn scurrying to move out of her way.

"I'd have thought it was impossible to make this protection detail worse," Shawn said, keeping his voice low as Xavier passed by him, "but you always have been good at achieving the impossible."

Xavier growled before hurrying to catch up with Bria.

Chapter Twenty-Two

Whatever is going on between us now, it can't last.

Stupid. Stupid. Stupid. That's exactly what she was for entertaining the idea that somehow she and Xavier could find their way back to each other. For thinking that he'd even want to. He saw the night they'd spent in bed together as nothing more than fun rolls in the hay for old times' sake and she'd been envisioning white picket fences. It sounded like the kind of script she'd toss in the garbage bin after the first five pages.

At least now she knew how he felt. It was ironic when she thought about it. She'd pushed him away fifteen years ago to pursue her dreams, and now he was pushing her away. Karma really was something else.

Well, she hadn't been voted People's Choice Awards' best actress twice in a row for nothing. She pushed her shoulders back farther and kept her eyes trained on the streets of Manhattan. She might have been heartbroken on the inside, nearly falling apart with grief for the future she'd already begun spinning in her head, but she wasn't about to show it on the outside.

Xavier pulled into a space in the small parking lot next to the set.

"Bria, I'm sorry about what I said back at the office. I was just—"

She held up a hand, cutting him off. "No need to apologize. I totally understand." She opened the passenger door and stepped out.

Xavier got out and hurried to her side, a frown on his face. "You're supposed to wait until I come around the car."

"I'm sorry. I forgot. I'm running a little late though, so could we hurry?"

She moved past him toward her dressing room. She stopped at the door. The room was big as far as dressing rooms went, but way too small for her and Xavier and all the emotions she had swirling inside. If he came in with her, there was no way she wasn't going to erupt and she had too much pride to let him see her fall apart over him.

She turned to face him. "The scene we're shooting this afternoon is important. I need to concentrate and prepare. Would you mind waiting out here?"

A part of her felt like a heel for even asking. A diva too special to let the hired help inside her precious space. The other side of her screamed to get away from Xavier if only for a little while. The screams won out.

The frown on his face deepened. "Fine," he spat. "I'll need to check out the interior first though."

She stepped aside to let him pass into the dressing room.

He was back in less than a minute. "It's clean."

"Thank you."

She showered and headed over to wardrobe and makeup with Xavier's words still echoing in her head. The fact that he trailed behind her the whole time made the words that much louder in her mind. But she pushed them aside when she was called to set and did her job. She'd always had the ability to get outside herself and into the role she was playing. It was one of the reasons she was so good at what she did. She was happy to see that her personal drama with Xavier hadn't changed that.

She managed to complete the scene in only three takes and headed back to wardrobe to change. Once again, Xavier waited outside her dressing room as she gathered her things. She took her time. It was hard enough riding in the same car with Xavier after hearing what he thought of their relationship. Or lack thereof. Spending another night under the same roof… She didn't think her heart could stand it.

He'd offered to take her to a safe house when she initially hired West Investigations and that seemed like the best option now, given the changed circumstances. Maybe Shawn or one of the other operatives could stay with her. She knew Xavier would resist the suggestion, but she was the client. If she insisted, Ryan West would have no choice but to go along with her desires.

Now she just had to tell Xavier.

She steeled herself and stepped out of the dressing room.

Xavier fell in step beside her after she locked the door and headed for the parking lot.

"I think it would be best if Ryan assigned someone else to my protection detail."

"No."

"You don't get to decide. I'm the client."

"You aren't just a client and you know it. I'm sorry about what I said. I didn't intend for you to hear it."

"That, I got," she scoffed.

"That's not what I meant," he growled.

They passed the security checkpoint and entered the parking lot. There were several more vehicles in the makeshift area now than there had been when they'd arrived.

"It doesn't matter. You can't control how you feel. I get that. But neither can I. Seeing you again, being with you again, it's brought up a lot of emotions I thought I'd dealt with a long time ago. But that's not your problem. If you don't feel the same way, then you don't."

Xavier laid a hand on her arm, gently stopping

her from moving forward. "I didn't say I didn't feel something for you."

"But not enough." She turned her face away from him so he couldn't see the tears that were threatening to fall although her voice was thick with them.

"I—"

The rest of his words were caught in the sound of an explosion that rocked the light blue sedan parked several spaces away.

Not far enough away to keep the blast from lifting her and Xavier from their feet and flinging them backward, across the parking lot.

Bria landed on the asphalt, pain reverberating throughout her entire body. Darkness swelled behind her eyes and she knew she was only seconds away from losing consciousness.

She turned her head, looking for Xavier, her fear for him palpable despite the pain she was in.

What she saw sent terror shooting through her alongside the pain.

Eliot.

He was beside her, lifting her into his arms.

"You're mine. Everything is going to be okay now."

Those were the last words she heard before the darkness claimed her.

Chapter Twenty-Three

"I need to get out of here. Now," Xavier said, struggling into a sitting position in the hospital bed.

He reached for his IV line but the nurse grabbed his hand before he could rip it out of his arm. "Mr. Nichols, you can't leave yet. You were unconscious for several minutes. The doctor has ordered a CT scan."

"I don't care what the doctor ordered. I'm leaving." He'd awoken in the back of an ambulance on the way to the hospital. If he could have, he'd have forced them to turn around and take him back to the movie set. He didn't have time for a hospital visit. He needed to find Bria.

"Xavier, listen to the lady." A voice boomed from the door.

Ryan strode into the room, followed closely by Shawn. The brothers wore matching expressions of concern on their faces.

"Sykes has Bria. Do you have a line on where he's taken her?" Xavier shot the question at Ryan.

"Not yet. But the police have put out a BOLO on

Eliot and his vehicle, and West has employed all of our resources. We will find them."

"The panic button," he said, desperation lacing each word.

Shawn shook his head. "She hasn't hit the button."

Xavier's heart leaped with fear. He had no doubt that West and the police were doing everything they could, but would it be enough?

The brothers shared a glance.

"What? What aren't you saying?" Xavier demanded.

"The cops also went to Sykes's apartment. The doorman said Sykes hasn't been there in a couple days and the building's management wouldn't let them into the place."

"Okay, so they need to get a warrant."

Ryan and Shawn glanced at each other again.

"Spit it out," Xavier growled through his teeth.

"There's only your word that Sykes took Bria and you were half-unconscious," Ryan said. "The police say they don't have enough to formally open an investigation into Sykes for kidnapping, and without it, they can't get a warrant to search his apartment."

He squelched the urge to bellow. Instead, he pointed to the IV and trained his gaze on the nurse. "Take it out now or I will pull it out."

The nurse studied him, ostensibly gauging just how serious he was. He reached for the line again.

"Okay, okay." She went to work taking the line out of his arm. "But if you are going to leave, you'll have to sign a paper saying you left against medical advice."

"I'll sign whatever you want, but you better bring it now. I've got work to do."

"Dude, you aren't going to be any help to anyone if you pass out," Shawn said. "Do what the doctors say and let us handle finding Sykes."

Xavier glared at the two men. "Would you, if it was Addy out there somewhere with a deranged man?" He looked at Ryan. "Or Nadia?"

His friends stayed silent.

"Exactly."

The nurse finished removing the IV. "Stay here. I'll be right back with the AMA form."

He was itching to get out of the hospital and start searching for Bria, but he nodded. Two minutes. That was all he was giving her before he took off. Long enough to put on his shoes, if he could find them.

He rose as the nurse left the room and headed for the closet. Luckily, he'd come to before they'd taken his clothes off him so he didn't have to worry about walking out of the hospital in a gown.

"What do we know so far?" He opened the closet door and found his shoes, watch, wallet and cell phone on the shelf inside in a large clear plastic bag.

He reached up, stifling a groan and fighting back dizziness.

Shawn gently nudged him out of the way and grabbed the bag. "The camera facing the parking lot caught the explosion, but we can't see you or Bria." Shawn carried the bag with his things back to the bed while Xavier followed at a slightly slower pace.

"Did anyone on set see anything? Which direction Sykes took off in, maybe? The make and model of the car? Anything?"

Ryan shook his head. "At the moment, it looks like you and Bria were the only ones in or around the parking area. The cops are questioning everyone on set at the time of the explosion."

Xavier sat much more slowly than he'd have liked and put on his shoes. "The cops aren't going to tell us anything even if they happen to get something from a witness."

"I know that." Ryan frowned. "Which is why I've also got people asking questions. We have to be discreet though, given we don't have any power or jurisdiction. But everyone on set knows that you were protecting Bria and so far people have been forthcoming."

"They just don't know anything," Xavier snapped, the frustration and fear bubbling in his chest.

"I sent Gideon to keep an eye on Sykes's place in case he shows up."

"Fine." Xavier finally finished lacing his boots and stood. "He can help me search Sykes's apartment when I get there."

"Let's just slow down a minute," Ryan said, stepping in front of Xavier.

"Let's not slow down," Xavier barked. "We don't know what that maniac is doing to her right now." He paused to swallow back the emotion that had swelled in his chest and throat. "I'm not waiting another minute before doing everything I can to find her. Now help me or get the hell out of my way."

Ryan blew out a deep breath before stepping aside. He and Shawn fell into step beside Xavier as they made their way down the hospital corridor, only stopping briefly at the nurses' station so that Xavier could sign himself out of the hospital against doctors' orders.

Shawn drove and they made good time getting from the hospital to Sykes's Chelsea apartment. Shawn illegally parked the SUV a block from the building and they walked back.

Gideon met them in front of the building's revolving glass doors. "The doorman agreed to let you go up to Sykes's apartment. You only have five minutes."

Shawn's eyebrows rose. "How did you manage that?"

A ghost of a smile crossed Gideon's lips. "The old-fashioned way. A bribe."

Gideon resumed his post outside the apartment, keeping an eye out in case Sykes showed up while the rest of them marched into the lobby and past the doorman who barely spared them a glance. They were silent on the elevator up to the eleventh floor.

Shawn picked the lock on the door and they were

inside Sykes's apartment within a minute of stepping out of the elevator.

"Careful," Ryan warned. "If the cops ever do get a warrant, we don't want them to know we were here."

The apartment wasn't large and the decor was minimal. The four of them split up with Shawn taking the living/dining/kitchen combination, Ryan taking the second bedroom, and Xavier heading for the main suite.

A king-size bed with a leather headboard sat against one wall, facing a sleek, black wall-mounted television. The bedside tables were empty and the closet and single dresser in the room held nothing other than clothing.

Xavier crossed the room into the adjoining bathroom. Another door on the other side of the room opened into the hallway. He found cleaners and a sponge under the sink but nothing that would lead them to where Sykes might be holding Bria.

"Xavier, Shawn," Ryan called. "In here."

Xavier entered the room behind Shawn and pulled up short. Ryan had the closet doors open. The walls inside were covered in photos of Bria. Some of them were of her in Los Angeles, while others had been taken more recently in New York. There were even a few of him and Bria together.

The pictures made his blood boil, but he tried to focus on what they might tell them about Sykes and where he could be.

"He's obsessed with her," Xavier whispered.

He stepped forward, examining the photos more closely. A knot formed in his stomach. Several had been taken through the windows of Bria's townhouse, likely with a long-range lens but still too close for his comfort.

"Nothing here tells us where Sykes has taken Bria." Xavier slammed his palm against the open closet door.

"Maybe there is. Look at this." Shawn held a notebook open, flipping through the pages. "I found it under the bed."

Ryan and Xavier each took a side and looked over Shawn's shoulder.

The notebook was full of Sykes's fantasies about the life he and Bria would live together.

"Here." Shawn turned the page and pointed. A photograph of a farmhouse had been taped onto one page above more ramblings about Sykes and Bria going somewhere where it would be just the two of them.

"Doesn't look like there's an address visible."

Xavier reached over Shawn's shoulder and pulled the photo out of the book, hoping to find an address or some writing on the back that would tell them where to find the house. There was nothing.

It took all his strength not to rip the photo into tiny pieces.

"If Sykes owns this place, it's not under his own name," Shawn said.

"Look under the name Morgan Ryder. He may have inherited it, so we should also look under his parents' names and any siblings' or any other family members'."

"I'll call into the office as soon as we're back in the car," Ryan said. "We should get out of here. We've already spent more than the five minutes Gideon paid for." He laid a hand on Xavier's shoulder. "We will find her."

Chapter Twenty-Four

Bria woke on an unfamiliar sofa, in an unfamiliar room. She had no idea how long she'd been unconscious, but she could see through the large window in front of the sofa that she was lying on that it was dark outside. The moon was bright though, so she could see that there was nothing beyond the window but a large lawn that ended where a copse of trees began.

Her head throbbed. She lifted her hands to her head and found that they'd been tied.

Xavier.

He'd been beside her when the car exploded. Where was he now? And was he okay?

He had to be. There was so much she hadn't said. So much time they'd wasted.

She pushed herself into a sitting position. Someone groaned. It took a moment before she realized that someone was her. Her entire body ached, almost enough to outweigh the fear coursing through her. Almost.

Eliot stepped into her sight line. "You're awake.

Good." The smile she'd once found charming looked grotesque now. "I made us a romantic dinner to celebrate the first night of our new life together."

Fear clouded her already foggy brain. Eliot was her stalker. He was delusional. Dangerous.

She had to break through his delusions. Get him to let her go.

"Eliot, I think I need a doctor. I need you to take me to the hospital."

Eliot went to his knees in front of the sofa. "You bumped your head. I got you two aspirin. I'll take care of you." He reached out and pushed a lock of hair off her forehead.

She fought against the desire to shrink away from his touch. Swallowing her revulsion, she said, "I think I need a doctor. Please, Eliot."

He pushed to his feet as if he hadn't heard her at all. "After you've taken your pills, I'll help you to the dining room. Everything is ready."

There was no way she was going to swallow any pills he was offering her. Her head was pounding, but right now what she needed more than anything was for it to clear. "I don't think I need aspirin. My head is feeling better."

Eliot grinned. "That's great. Let's eat, then."

He reached for her arm and helped her get to her feet. She wobbled but found her footing quickly. Eliot didn't let go of her arm. They moved into the formal dining room. Eliot had set the table with two elaborate place settings complete with salad and bread plates and crystal. Her eyes glanced over the silverware. He'd set a fork by her place setting, but only his had a knife. Of course, it would be a lot easier to use them to defend herself if her hands weren't tied.

She hoped it wouldn't come to that. Eliot was clearly not in his right mind, but maybe she could talk him back into his senses. Make him see that this was not the way to win her love.

He pulled out a chair for her at the table and she sat.

The change in position drew her attention to something in her pocket.

Her panic button.

If she could get her hand into her pocket and hit the button without Eliot seeing, Xavier would know exactly where she was.

She held her still tied hands out in front of her. "I can't eat with my hands tied."

Eliot had already placed the food, in covered dishes, at the center of the table.

"Yes, you can." Eliot reached for the open bottle of red wine on the table between them and poured them each a glass. "I'll help you. It will be romantic. I can feed you."

Her stomach turned. So he wasn't going to untie her. Fine. She could still hit the button. Maybe without even reaching into her pockets. The fabric of her slacks wasn't that heavy.

She shifted her hands back into her lap in what she hoped was a pose that looked casual to Eliot. He didn't seem to be watching her closely at all, lost in what he imagined was some sort of romantic dinner. And where did he think this romantic dinner would lead?

The thought sent a shudder through her. She moved her hands toward her left pocket.

Eliot stood. He whipped the covers off the platters on the table with a flourish, revealing a roast and vegetables. He sliced the roast, then doled out food onto each of their plates before sitting down again.

"Now, isn't this lovely? I can't tell you how long I've waited for us to be together like this. No agents, no fans, no costars. Just the two of us, the way it should have been since *Murder in Cabin Nine*." Eliot reached across the table and used his knife to cut her meat.

She recoiled, not wanting him near her with a knife in his hand. Or at all.

Eliot frowned.

She plastered a smile on her face and tried to look as if she'd moved just to give him more room to slice her food. It seemed to work. In more ways than one.

Eliot returned her smile, but she was more concerned with the fact that the shift in her body allowed her easier access to the panic button. She pressed the button through the material of her slacks, feeling the small fob pressing into her leg.

Please work. Please work.

"I know you had a part in *Murder in Cabin Nine*."

"You were so nice to me. I've never forgotten that, although I know you didn't remember who I was."

"I'm sorry I didn't remember you. Is that why you've done all this? Because I didn't remember you?"

The look he gave her reflected genuine shock. "Of course not! I mean, I've loved you since we met on set, but I totally understood you had to focus on your career. I don't hold your ambition against you."

The way he spoke, as if they'd had some type of relationship that didn't solely exist in his mind, sent a shiver through her. But she wanted to keep him talking. It might be the only way to bring him back to reality.

"I think we should spend some time together, just the two of us, laying a strong foundation for our relationship going forward, but after a few years, I wouldn't have any problem with you going back to work. I mean, it would be a shame to let everything I've done to further your career go to waste."

Eliot giggled as if he was in on a secret that she wasn't.

A sinking feeling in her gut said he wasn't just talking about the public relations work he'd done for her. "Are you talking about your PR work?"

He giggled again. "That's just the little stuff." He leaned across the table, all wide grin and wild eyes. "I killed Derek Longwell."

Bria sucked in a sharp breath, but Eliot didn't seem to notice.

"I saw what he did to you. Well, I saw him on top of you in the woods and you hit him with a rock. Good girl." His smile was grotesque. "You ran away, but Derek was stunned. When he saw me approaching he barked at me to help him. I helped him all right. I picked up the rock you'd hit him with and hit him again. It only took one blow."

Bile rose in Bria's throat despite her empty stomach.

"And Bernie? Did you kill him too?" She knew the answer, but something compelled her to hear it directly from Eliot.

He nodded, spearing a bit of potato and meat with his fork and popping it into his mouth. "He was easy." Eliot spoke around the food in his mouth. "I'd been keeping tabs on your place. I saw that bodyguard of yours get into it with Bernie. Bernie had no right to follow you like that," Eliot said with a frown and no hint of irony. "Taking pictures of you everywhere you went. Invading your privacy."

"Why did you leave Bernie's body in front of my house?"

Eliot's head dipped and he looked at her out of the side of his eye, shyly. "I wanted you to know what I was willing to do for you. How much I loved you. I didn't tell you about Derek and that was a mistake. I wasn't going to make that mistake again."

He'd let his delusions get the best of him, but this was not the moment to tell him that.

"So everything…the emails, the flowers. You killed Bernie. You did it all?"

"For you," he said. "I followed you to New York to keep an eye on you while you were filming. I wanted to be close to you. I always want to be close to you."

How had she missed it? Eliot had lost all connection with reality.

"Eliot, you know I care for you and respect you as a friend."

He kept cutting as if he hadn't heard her.

"This isn't the way to get me to fall in love with you. You need to let me go."

"Why? So you can run into the arms of that bodyguard of yours? Do you really think I don't know that you're sleeping with him?"

She sucked in a deep breath. She hadn't thought twice about having Eliot over to her apartment in Los Angeles or the townhouse in New York. Had he planted some kind of listening or video devices? No, no, he couldn't have. And even if he had, she and Xavier had been together at his house not hers. Still, the thought of Eliot somehow watching them, even if he hadn't had a view inside their homes, was sickening.

A deep scowl twisted his lips. "I see I hit the nail on the head." He stuttered out a deep breath. "It's okay. I can forgive you one indiscretion. As long as it never happens again, of course."

"That's why you sent me that photograph and the threats against Xavier. You wanted to frighten him away from me."

He scoffed. "I should have known better. A meathead like him. All brawn and no brains. I should have just killed him like I killed Bernie."

Eliot sawed her meat faster.

The words coming out of his mouth were terrifying but not nearly as much as the knife in his hand. "Eliot," she said in a voice she hoped was soothing. "We can work this out. Just untie me."

The knife slid off the plate, and Eliot's hand hit her wineglass sending it toppling over. Red wine spread across the white lace tablecloth.

Eliot surged to his feet, throwing the fork and knife down on the table. "Look what you made me do! I wanted our first dinner as a couple to be perfect." His eyes flashed with anger.

Terror swelled in Bria's chest. She cut her gaze up at him.

He reached down and yanked her to her feet, pulling her to his chest. "Now you'll have to pay for that."

Chapter Twenty-Five

Xavier's heart hadn't stopped beating as if it would pop out of his chest at any moment since he regained consciousness and realized Bria was gone. It had already been nearly four hours, and with each passing moment, he found it harder to breathe. Sykes could have taken her anywhere in four hours.

Focus.

He, Shaw and Ryan returned to West Investigations' headquarters while Gideon remained at Sykes's building, keeping lookout. Now they sat in the conference room, awash in the information that West's researchers had been able to find on Eliot Sykes, aka Morgan Ryder. In his early twenties, Sykes had embarked on a middling acting career that included only one credit for a deodorant commercial. They'd been able to turn up a couple of Morgan Ryder's headshots. The man in the photograph was definitely a younger Eliot Sykes. Tate Harwood had also been able to dig up a thin file on Sykes from his work on *Murder in Cabin Nine*, which had included Sykes's application for the production assistant's job. He'd listed his older brother, Joseph, as his emergency contact, and Ryan was working on finding contact information for him now, but he was apparently doing a stint with Doctors Without Borders so it was slow going.

The police weren't telling them anything officially, but Brandon was using his police contacts to funnel information to them unofficially. Unfortunately, the cops hadn't made any more progress on finding Bria than he had. Where was she?

Xavier pushed the file he was reading away and let his head fall into his hands.

"Hey, why don't you take a break?" Shawn dropped a hand on his shoulder and squeezed.

"I can't." Xavier reached for the background report on Sykes again. "There has to be something in here that gives us a clue to where he's taken Bria."

Excited voices mingled with hurried footsteps in the hall. Ryan and Tess burst into the room.

"Bria activated her panic button," Ryan said.

Xavier pushed to his feet and dashed around to the other side of the table where Tess had sat the laptop she'd carried into the room.

"She's too far away to get an exact location but we can tell the general area. She's, or at least the panic button's signal, is in Putnam County about an hour and ten minutes away," Tess said.

"I've already got Gideon on his way and we'll let the cops know when we're en route," Ryan said, falling in step beside Xavier as he headed from the room. "The signal should get more precise as we get closer to the button's location."

"Good," Xavier said, forgoing the elevators and pushing through the door to the stairwell.

Ryan grabbed his arm, forcing him to stop. "Are you sure you're up for this? I can't have you running on pure emotion. I need to know your head is on straight."

He understood where Ryan was coming from. He'd be no good to Bria and a potential danger to Ryan and whoever else was at his back if he couldn't rein in his emotions and think rationally.

He took a deep breath and let it out. "I can do this."

Ryan nodded, but Xavier read hesitancy in his eyes.

Xavier was able to cut the hour-and-ten-minute drive down to something closer to forty minutes. They kept Tess on the speaker, giving them updates on the panic button's location.

"Damn," Tess's anxious voice carried through the SUV's speakers.

"What is it, Tess?" Ryan said.

"The GPS in the panic button just went offline."

Xavier's heart thundered. "What does that mean?"

"We lost the signal."

Ryan swore.

Xavier was too terrified to react. If they couldn't follow the panic button's signal, they had no idea where to look for Bria.

"Have we found any connection between Sykes and a house, a business, a shed, anything out here in Putnam County?" Ryan barked.

"Nothing yet. We're still looking though," Tess responded.

Xavier wracked his brain. There had to be a way to locate Bria. He couldn't get this close and fail her. "I've got the photo of the farmhouse on my phone," he said, an idea blossoming in his head.

He navigated the SUV into a hard right turn, bouncing into the parking lot of a combination convenience store and gas station.

Ryan slanted a glance across the car at him. "What are you doing?"

"We need to know where that farmhouse is. That's the best lead we have to where Sykes might be holding Bria and since the panic button's GPS leads us to this area, it stands to reason it's located somewhere near here."

Xavier swung into a parking space and slammed the car into park. "When you're lost you ask for directions. We show the photo around and ask if anyone can direct us to it."

He hopped out of the car with Ryan on his heels.

The man behind the counter inside the convenience store looked up as they entered. "Hello, can I help you find something?"

"I'm hoping you can." Ryan took the lead. He pulled the photo of the house up on his phone. "We're trying to get to this house, but our GPS has died and we don't have the exact address. Do you recognize it?"

The man's eyes narrowed with suspicion. "I'm not sure."

Xavier reigned in his frustration. "Sir, a woman has been kidnapped. She's being held in this house." He tapped the phone's screen. "If you know where this house is, please help us find her."

The man studied them for a long moment. "Are you cops?"

Xavier and Ryan shared a glance.

"No," Ryan answered. "We're private investigators and friends of the woman who has been kidnapped."

"PIs." The man's expression morphed from suspicion to eagerness. "I always wondered what it was like to be a PI. Like that *Magnum PI*, you remember the old show?"

"Sir, please," Xavier pressed. "The house. Do you know where it is?"

The man sighed. "It looks like the old Dobrinsky place although no Dobrinsky has owned it for more than thirty years. People around here still call it that though."

"Do you know who owns it now?" Ryan pressed.

"Um…some doctor and his family bought it way back when."

Xavier shot a look at Ryan. Sykes's father and brother were doctors.

"No one has lived in the house for years now though. Not since the old doctor died. I guess his wife, if she's still alive, or his kids own it now."

"How do we get to the house from here?" Xavier asked, impatiently.

The man frowned but gave them the address for the house and sketched a map out on a napkin.

Ryan threw a hurried thank-you over his shoulder as they ran back to the car.

Xavier gunned the SUV in the direction the man had told them to go, while Ryan called Gideon and Tess to give them the house's location.

Since Xavier wasn't about to allow the fact that they had no legal authority to go after Sykes stop them, he, Ryan and Tess decided on the drive up that Tess would call the local police once they'd safely rescued Bria.

Xavier spied the semi-obscured driveway that the convenience store clerk said led to the farmhouse. He could see how they could have had trouble with the GPS tracker in Bria's panic button. The house was almost completely obscured by trees. There was no way they'd have seen the structure simply driving by. From the looks of it, the property encompassed several acres. Which also meant that there could be other buildings on the property where Sykes was holding Bria. Buildings it would take time to find and clear. Time Bria might not have.

Xavier stopped the car and cut the engine as soon

as the house came into view. He and Ryan stepped out of the SUV just as Gideon pulled to a stop behind them.

They met in the space between the two vehicles.

"Gideon, you go around the back," Ryan said, pulling his gun from its holster. "Xavier and I will enter through the front."

They crept toward the farmhouse. The exterior confirmed the convenience store clerk's statements about the home having been sitting vacant for an extended period. The lawn was overgrown and the siding needed to be replaced in several places. The stairs leading to the porch were crumbling and several shutters were missing from the front windows.

Gideon cut across the lawn and headed for the back of the house.

Xavier and Ryan waited several moments, giving Gideon the opportunity to get into place before they moved up the crumbling stairs to take position on either side of the front door.

"Ready?" Ryan whispered.

Xavier said a quick prayer that they'd find Bria inside and safe, then nodded.

"On three," Ryan said. "One, two, three!"

Chapter Twenty-Six

"You need to understand that you are mine!" Eliot's face twisted with rage. "I love you."

"You killed two people. You blew up a car and kidnapped me. That's not love."

Eliot's eyes darkened. He let out a scream that felt as if it shook the foundation of the house.

Bria's heart thundered in her chest. There was no reasoning with Eliot. He was lost in the delusion he'd created for himself.

Her hands were still bound, but she lunged for the table and grabbed the knife. In one quick motion, she turned back to Eliot and slashed it across his face.

Blood spilled from the wound and Eliot howled, hitting her across the cheek and sending her tumbling into the back of her chair. The knife fell from her hand and slid under the table, out of reach. Luckily, she managed to stay on her feet.

"You bitch!" Eliot pressed the palm of his hand to the wound on his face and glared at her. "I'll kill you."

He took a step toward her, but she lowered her

head and drove her body into his chest, sending him reeling backward.

Bria kept moving forward, past him and out of the dining room.

The layout of the house was a mystery to her, but she'd seen a set of stairs from the living room sofa when she'd regained consciousness and she headed that way now.

The hallway was pitch-black, which was a double-edged sword. On the one hand, it made it harder for Eliot to see, but it also made it harder for her to see. Presumably Eliot knew the layout of the house so the advantage went to him. The hallway was long and curved. She tried the doors lining it, finding the first two locked.

She ran for the third door, as the sound of Eliot's footsteps trailed down the corridor. The door opened without a sound and she darted into the room, turning the flimsy lock, despite knowing it wouldn't stop Eliot if he really wanted in.

"Bria. Oh, Briiiiiiaaaaa." Eliot called out her name in a singsong voice. She could hear what sounded like the handle on one of the other bedroom doors being jiggled and then footsteps moving again.

She worked her wrists in hopes of loosening the ropes enough to slip them free, as her eyes darted over the room searching for something to use as a weapon. There was nothing in the room except a bed, stripped down to the bare mattress, and a dresser. She considered for a moment, searching in the dresser drawers, but rejected the idea as the footsteps in the hall drew louder and closer. It didn't seem like Eliot was forcing the locked bedroom doors open. Not yet, at least. And as long as he wasn't, she had time to come up with a plan.

"Come out, come out, wherever you are," Eliot sang. "Really, Bria, I'm tired of this game. Why don't you come on out here and we can talk about this like adults. I can be reasonable."

The handle on the door to the room she was hiding in moved up and down. There was nothing but a thin piece of wood separating her from Eliot and she was terrified he could hear her thundering heart.

After what seemed like an eternity, she heard his footsteps continue down the hall, away from the door. She let out the breath she'd been holding. She couldn't hide in this room forever. Eventually, Eliot would start forcing the locks and there wasn't even a closet in the room that she could hide inside of.

She was finally able to loosen the knot on the rope Eliot had tied her hands with enough to slip one of her hands, and then the other, free. Ugly red marks marred her skin, but at least now she'd be able to fight back.

She had to move. Back toward the living room and presumably a door. She didn't know where they were exactly, but Eliot had to have driven her here, so there must be a road somewhere nearby. She just had to get to it and hitch a ride with a passerby to a nearby town or police station. And all while avoiding Eliot. It wouldn't be easy but the alternative…

She shuddered.

More footsteps and the squeak of the floorboards sounded faintly from down the hall. And then another sound, rusted door hinges being forced open. Apparently, Eliot had found an unlocked room. There wasn't likely to be a better time.

Bria eased the door open and peeked into the hall. It was empty but a door at the far end stood open. It was now or never.

She slipped from the bedroom and ran as quickly and quietly as she could back toward the front of the house. But not quietly enough. She threw a glance over her shoulder just in time to see Eliot step into the hallway.

Their eyes met as she turned the corner and raced out of the hall.

Eliot bounded after her.

Bria fled down the stairs and past the dining room and through the living room, past the sofa that she'd woken up on. Just beyond the living room was another hallway that split in two different directions. She had no idea which way led to the door and no time to figure it out.

She lurched to the right.

"Bria!" Eliot thundered behind her.

Her lungs burned, but hope swelled in her chest

when the large front door came into view. She grabbed the handle and pulled, but it didn't budge. She flicked the lock and still nothing happened.

Eliot must have done something to keep it from opening.

She turned, looking for another exit.

Eliot stood at the fork in the hallway.

His gaze sent ice through her veins. There was no doubt in her mind he was going to kill her.

Unfortunately, there was only one direction to go in, and it required heading back toward the stairs. Well, she wasn't going to go without a fight.

Bria gave a primal scream and raced at him. A look of surprise colored Eliot's face as she threw herself into him and they both hit the floor hard.

She'd trained six days a week, weights, cardio and some martial arts, while she was filming the Princess Kaleva movies. She reached for that training now, throwing punch after punch to Eliot's face and neck. She heard a crunch as one of her blows made contact. A satisfying gush of blood flowed from his nose.

She scrambled to her feet.

But Eliot recovered fast. He pushed to his feet, driving his shoulder into her stomach as he rose.

The attack stole the breath from her lungs, sending her wobbling on her feet.

Eliot's arm whipped out and around in a circular motion, connecting with Bria's jaw. Tears swam in her eyes and she fell to her knees.

Don't lose consciousness. She fought against the desire to go to sleep. Every instinct in her body said that if she did, she'd likely never wake up. She shook the drowsiness off in time to see Eliot's foot kick out.

Surprising herself she caught his leg before it made contact with her ribs.

Shock flashed across his face when she yanked with all the strength she had. Shock turned to surprise as he realized he was losing his balance.

She scrambled to her feet as he hit the floor on his back and ran for the dining room. There had to be a kitchen in the house. Hopefully, it led to a back door, and if not, she'd at least be able to grab a weapon to defend herself.

She made it to the living room before Eliot tackled her from behind. She landed on the hardwood floors hard enough to rattle her teeth.

He flung her onto her back.

She reached for the wound on his face, scratching at it, his eyes, wherever she could reach. He yelled in pain, then grabbed her by the hair, slamming her head into the floor.

Bria's ears rang and her vision swam. She tried to focus, to make her body move, but the signals weren't getting from her terrified brain to her limbs. She couldn't just lie there. She had to keep trying. She needed to stay alive until Xavier found her.

It took every bit of strength she had, but she managed to flip onto her stomach and begin crawling away from Eliot. The room spun, but she could make out the long hallway she'd been headed for when he'd tackled her.

"I thought you were the one." Eliot's voice came from behind her. She glanced over her shoulder and saw that he was standing in the middle of the room, watching her, tears falling from his eyes. The sight was equal parts pitiful and petrifying.

She moved faster and the front door of the house came into view.

Eliot's footfalls sounded behind her.

He yanked her to her feet just as the door crashed open.

Xavier stood in the doorway, his gun held outstretched.

Eliot's arm came around Bria's throat, cutting off most of her air supply.

"Let her go," Xavier demanded.

"No! She's mine. We belong together." Eliot took several steps back, dragging her along with him.

Xavier stepped farther into the house, followed by Ryan West. Both men had their guns pointed at her and Eliot. But she knew they wouldn't shoot. She was in the way.

She heard a door burst open somewhere behind her.

"You've got nowhere to go, Eliot. We've got you surrounded. Let her go and we can talk about all of this. If you hurt her, you're a dead man."

Eliot's arm tightened around her neck and he dragged her back several more steps.

Xavier and his men hadn't heard Eliot earlier. They didn't know that there was no chance that he'd give up. He'd see them both killed first.

Bria could feel herself getting light-headed. She didn't have long before she passed out, and who knew what Eliot would do then. She needed to do something to get herself out of the line of fire.

She lowered her head and bit down on Eliot's forearm.

He yowled and loosened his grip enough that she could slip under it. She launched herself away from Eliot.

Xavier and Ryan thundered forward, barking at Eliot to get onto his knees, while Gideon rounded on Eliot from the kitchen. It must have been him she'd heard bursting into the house from the back door.

Eliot reached behind him and a shard of light glinted off the knife as he whipped it forward toward Xavier.

The gunshot thundered through the room.

Eliot froze, the knife still outstretched. He looked down at his stomach where blood had already begun blooming over his shirt. He stumbled, then collapsed.

Ryan rushed forward, grabbing Eliot's hands and placing them in cuffs while the third man kept his gun trained on Eliot.

Xavier hurried to Bria's side and pulled her into his arms. "Baby, are you okay?"

She looked into his eyes and told the truth. "No." Her hands trembled, adrenaline still surging through her body. "Is he dead?" She tried to peer over Xavier's shoulder to get a look at Eliot, but he shifted, making it impossible for her to see past him.

She could hear Ryan on the phone with 9-1-1, asking for an ambulance immediately. Eliot must still be alive. She wasn't sure if she was relieved or not.

She wrapped her arms around Xavier, pulling him close and burying her face in his chest.

"It's over. You're safe now."

And for the first time in months, she actually felt like that might be the truth.

Chapter Twenty-Seven

Bria watched through the tinted windows as Xavier made his way over to the SUV from the front of the police cruiser where he'd been speaking to the Putnam County police detectives. They had not been happy to discover that Xavier and his men had taken it upon themselves to rescue her instead of alerting their department. The detectives still weren't happy, but her statement describing her kidnapping and Eliot's loud and unhinged ravings that she was his, had done a lot to neutralize the tempers of the local cops. It had also helped that West Investigations had implied that they'd let the Putnam County chief of police take credit for having saved Hollywood's darling from the stalker who'd kidnapped her.

Xavier opened the back door of the SUV and slid in beside Bria. She had the heat cranked up and a blanket wrapped around her shoulders, but she didn't begin to feel warm until he wrapped his arms around her.

They held each other for several minutes before pulling away.

"Is everything okay? Are you and your guys in trouble?" she asked.

Xavier shook his head. "I don't think so. At least, nothing major anyway. The chief is too busy dreaming about all the press he's going to get."

She let out a deep breath. "That's good, I guess."

"I don't like that he's trading on you being kidnapped to advance his career."

"I'm used to it. It's not just Hollywood that's cutthroat. If that's all it takes to keep you, Shawn and Gideon out of jail, I'm happy to let the cops have their fifteen minutes at my expense."

"Are you really okay?" Concern shone in Xavier's eyes.

He ran a finger over the bruise that was forming on her cheek. She had several other bumps and bruises from her fight with Eliot. They would take a few weeks to heal completely, but no permanent damage had been done, which was what she told the EMTs who had tried to take her to get checked out at the local hospital.

She didn't want to leave Xavier, and the police hadn't been through questioning him so she'd declined the offer.

She leaned her forehead against his. "I was terrified in that house with Eliot. But one thing I knew for sure was that you were looking for me and that you would move heaven and earth to find me. And you did."

"I will always be there for you when you need me. Always." He kissed her softly.

She was still struggling to process that Eliot, a man she'd considered a friend and trusted confidant, was her stalker. Xavier was right. She hadn't known Eliot at all. His delusions had run deep. The police had already discovered that Eliot had followed her to New York a few days after she'd crossed the country to start filming *Loss of Days*. He'd been the one delivering the flowers, and feeling threatened by Xavier's presence and the obvious feelings she had for him, he'd escalated his stalking.

"There's something I need to tell you." She'd promised herself that when she got out of that house and away from Eliot, she'd tell Xavier how she felt about him and she wasn't going to waste another moment before keeping that promise to herself.

"I let you go fifteen years ago without telling you how much you mean to me. I loved you then and I love you now. And I'm hoping it is not too late for us. I don't know exactly how we'd make it work, but I know I want to make it work with you and I'll do whatever it takes. Move to New York and commute back and forth to Los Angeles when I have to. Or I'll focus my career on projects that film on the East Coast. Whatever it takes. I just know that as hard as I've worked to become Brianna Baker, movie star, that's how hard I'm willing to work to build a relationship with you that lasts," she said pointedly, remembering what he'd told Ryan about their relationship not being meant to last.

"Bria, about what you overheard me say—"

She held up a hand. "I don't want to look back. Let's start from here. Committed to making us work. What do you say?"

She waited anxiously for what felt like hours until a wide grin began spreading across Xavier's face.

"I love you too."

She grinned. "You do?"

"I do." He grinned back. "And you don't have to change a thing."

Her heart beat fast. She was having trouble processing what he was saying beyond the joy she felt at hearing he loved her as much as she loved him. "Why? What do you mean I don't have to change a thing?"

"Ryan and Shawn have been planning to open a West Coast office for a while now and they offered me the job of heading it up some time ago."

"You mean you'd be willing to move to Los Angeles?" She could barely believe what she was hearing. She hadn't even considered that he'd move to be with her.

His smile grew wider. "I'd be more than willing. I don't care where I live as long as you're there too."

Love swelled in Bria's chest. She threw her arms around Xavier and kissed him with all the passion and yearning that had laid dormant in her heart for him over the last fifteen years and all the hope she had for the years to come.

Chapter Twenty-Eight

"I could get used to this life." Xavier stretched his arms over his head and burrowed further into the oversize deck chair next to her.

The Pacific Ocean stretched out in front of them as far as the eye could see. The breeze off the ocean cooled the sun's warm rays. She understood where Xavier was coming from, but a few days was all they could manage, budget wise and time wise.

Bria laughed. "I suggest you don't. Renting a yacht is okay for a couple days for our honeymoon, but we both have to go back to work eventually."

He reached across the short space separating their chairs and took her hand, turning it over and kissing her palm. Love tugged at his heart every time he saw his ring on her finger. It had been such a long road for them getting here. But here they were. Together, forever.

"I guess I'll just have to be content with a long weekend with my wife and the wide open sea."

"It's not so bad." She smiled at him and his heart fluttered.

"It's not bad at all."

And it wasn't, especially after everything they'd gone through in the last eight months. Eliot had insisted on going to trial on the stalking and murder charges. The case was a slam dunk for the prosecution. The cops had found the knife that had killed Bernie Steele in Eliot's apartment and they'd been able to find traces of Bernie's blood under the handle, even though the knife had been cleaned. He and Bria had been called to the stand as witnesses. Testifying had been especially difficult on Bria, who'd had to relive her kidnapping and being held captive by a man she'd thought of as her friend. They'd both been relieved when the jury had come back with guilty verdicts for Bria's kidnapping, Bernie's murder and a host of other charges. It wasn't clear that he'd ever be charged for Derek Longwell's murder, unfortunately. Eliot had insisted that Bria was lying about his having confessed to that murder, and given the years long lag and the shoddy police work that had been done back then, it was unlikely the prosecutors could get a conviction. Still, Eliot would be in jail for a very long time for the crimes he'd been convicted of, which was exactly where he belonged.

Xavier had wasted no time in asking Bria to marry him after the trial was officially over. He'd taken her out for a romantic dinner the very next day and proposed. And she'd accepted.

He'd have married her that night, but Bria had wanted a wedding, nothing big and definitely something private, but she'd wanted all their friends and family to know how much they loved each other. Their schedules had kept them too busy to plan a wedding. He'd moved across the country to California and had opened West Investigations' West Coast office. He was happy to say the new office was taking off, but it had been a lot of work in a short time.

And Bria had been traveling a lot promoting *Loss of Days*. The audiences and critics loved the movie and her performance in particular. She'd already been nominated for several awards and there were even whispers that she'd be nominated for an Oscar next year. They'd been ships passing in the night to some extent, but they'd made the most of the time they'd been able to spend together over the last several months.

Then, two days earlier, she'd surprised him by renting the yacht and proposing they have the boat's captain, who was also a justice of the peace, marry them at sea.

They'd exchanged vows the night before, under a setting sun, the first mate and the yacht chef acting as their witnesses.

It was perfect. Just like his wife.

"What are you thinking right now?" Bria asked.

He leaned over and kissed his bride. "How much I love you and how lucky we are to have found our way back to each other."

"I couldn't agree with you more."

* * * * *

Look for more books in K.D. Richards's ongoing West Investigations miniseries coming in 2024!

And be sure to look for the most recent title in the series, Under the Cover of Darkness, *available now wherever Harlequin books are sold!*

#2199 A PLACE TO HIDE
Lookout Mountain Mysteries • by Debra Webb

Two and a half years ago, Grace Myers, infant son in tow, escaped a serial killer. Now, she'll have to trust Deputy Robert Vaughn to safeguard their identities and lives. The culprit is still on the loose and determined to get even...

#2200 WETLANDS INVESTIGATION
The Swamp Slayings • by Carla Cassidy

Investigator Nick Cain is in the small town of Black Bayou for one reason— to catch a serial killer. But between his unwanted attraction to his partner Officer Sarah Beauregard and all the deadly town secrets he uncovers, will his plan to catch the killer implode?

#2201 K-9 DETECTION
New Mexico Guard Dogs • by Nichole Severn

Jocelyn Carville knows a dangerous cartel is responsible for the Alpine Valley PD station bombing. But convincing Captain Baker Halsey is harder than uncovering the cartel's motive. Until the syndicate's next attack makes their risky partnership inevitable...

#2202 SWIFTWATER ENEMIES
Big Sky Search and Rescue • by Danica Winters

When Aspen Stevens and Detective Leo West meet at a crime scene, they instantly dislike each other. But uncovering the truth about their victim means combining search and rescue expertise and acknowledging the fine line between love and hate even as they risk their lives...

#2203 THE PERFECT WITNESS
Secure One • by Katie Mettner

Security expert Cal Newfellow knows safety is an illusion. But when he's tasked with protecting Marlise, a prosecutor's star witness against an infamous trafficker and murderer, he'll do everything in his power to keep the danger—and his heart—away from her.

#2204 MURDER IN THE BLUE RIDGE MOUNTAINS
The Lynleys of Law Enforcement • by R. Barri Flowers

After a body is discovered in the mountains, special agent Garrett Sneed returns home to work the case with his ex, law enforcement ranger Madison Lynley. Before long, their attraction is heating up...until another homicide reveals a possible link to his mother's unsolved murder. And then the killer sets his sights on Madison...

Get 3 FREE REWARDS!

We'll send you 2 FREE Books <u>plus</u> a FREE Mystery Gift.

FREE Value Over **$20**

Both the **Harlequin Intrigue®** and **Harlequin® Romantic Suspense** series feature compelling novels filled with heart-racing action-packed romance that will keep you on the edge of your seat.

YES! Please send me 2 FREE novels from the Harlequin Intrigue or Harlequin Romantic Suspense series and my FREE gift (gift is worth about $10 retail). After receiving them, if I don't wish to receive any more books, I can return the shipping statement marked "cancel." If I don't cancel, I will receive 6 brand-new Harlequin Intrigue Larger-Print books every month and be billed just $6.49 each in the U.S. or $6.99 each in Canada, a savings of at least 13% off the cover price, or 4 brand-new Harlequin Romantic Suspense books every month and be billed just $5.49 each in the U.S. or $6.24 each in Canada, a savings of at least 12% off the cover price. It's quite a bargain! Shipping and handling is just 50¢ per book in the U.S. and $1.25 per book in Canada.* I understand that accepting the 2 free books and gift places me under no obligation to buy anything. I can always return a shipment and cancel at any time by calling the number below. The free books and gift are mine to keep no matter what I decide.

Choose one: ☐ **Harlequin Intrigue Larger-Print** (199/399 BPA GRMX) ☐ **Harlequin Romantic Suspense** (240/340 BPA GRMX) ☐ **Or Try Both!** (199/399 & 240/340 BPA GRQD)

Name (please print)

Address   Apt. #

City   State/Province   Zip/Postal Code

Email: Please check this box ☐ if you would like to receive newsletters and promotional emails from Harlequin Enterprises ULC and its affiliates. You can unsubscribe anytime.

Mail to the **Harlequin Reader Service:**
IN U.S.A.: P.O. Box 1341, Buffalo, NY 14240-8531
IN CANADA: P.O. Box 603, Fort Erie, Ontario L2A 5X3

Want to try 2 free books from another series! Call 1-800-873-8635 or visit www.ReaderService.com.

*Terms and prices subject to change without notice. Prices do not include sales taxes, which will be charged (if applicable) based on your state or country of residence. Canadian residents will be charged applicable taxes. Offer not valid in Quebec. This offer is limited to one order per household. Books received may not be as shown. Not valid for current subscribers to the Harlequin Intrigue or Harlequin Romantic Suspense series. All orders subject to approval. Credit or debit balances in a customer's account(s) may be offset by any other outstanding balance owed by or to the customer. Please allow 4 to 6 weeks for delivery. Offer available while quantities last.

Your Privacy—Your information is being collected by Harlequin Enterprises ULC, operating as Harlequin Reader Service. For a complete summary of the information we collect, how we use this information and to whom it is disclosed, please visit our privacy notice located at corporate.harlequin.com/privacy-notice. From time to time we may also exchange your personal information with reputable third parties. If you wish to opt out of this sharing of your personal information, please visit readerservice.com/consumerschoice or call 1-800-873-8635. **Notice to California Residents**—Under California law, you have specific rights to control and access your data. For more information on these rights and how to exercise them, visit corporate.harlequin.com/california-privacy.

HIHRS23